Valentines Day

TIME PATROL

BOB MAYER

Dedication

To The Dreamers Of The Night
Who Make Them A Reality In The Day

"The point in history at which we stand is full of promise and danger. The world will either move
forward toward unity and widely shared prosperity—or it will move apart."
President Franklin D. Roosevelt.

The Time Patrol

There once was a place called Atlantis. Ten thousand years ago it was attacked by a force known
only as the Shadow, on the same date, over the course of six years. The seventh attack led to
Atlantis being obliterated to the point where it is just a legend, but our ancestors managed to
survive.

There are many Earth timelines. The Shadow comes from one of those alternate timelines (or perhaps more than one). It is attacking our timeline by punching bubbles into our past that last no more than twenty-four hours. In each bubble, the Shadow is trying to change our history and cause a time ripple.

By itself, a single time ripple can be dealt with, corrected, and absorbed. But a significant time ripple that is unchecked can become a Cascade. That changes things, but the timeline still survives.

Six Cascades can combine to become a seventh event: a Time Tsunami.

That would be the end of our timeline and our existence.

To achieve its goal, the Shadow attacks six points in time simultaneously, the same date in different years.

The Time Patrol's job is to keep our timeline intact.

The Time Patrol sends an agent back to each of those bubbles in those six years to keep history the same.

This is one of those dates: **14 February**.

Popularly known as Valentines Day

Where The Time Patrol Ended Up
This Particular Day: 14 February

"You can accomplish more with a smile, a handshake, and a gun than you do with just a smile and handshake." Al Capone

Chicago, 14 February 1929 A.D.

It was not the best of times; the Time Patrol didn't go to those.

As usual, it was one of the worst of times to travel back to: grey weather, snowing outside, and Ivar was sitting at a table in a diner across from a psychopathic killer. Add to that the likelihood of seven deaths occurring later this morning if history played out as it should. And that was the reason Ivar was here; *and now.*

Ivar had never had a 'best of time' in his time traveling experiences when one adds up his trips, which include being fitted for cement shoes by Meyer Lansky in 1929 and getting caught in the Presidential Palace in the midst of the coup in 1973 Chile.

The psycho across the table spoke. "They call me Strings."

Ivar checked the implanted download but there was no mention of a Strings or an aka 'Strings' amongst either Al Capone's or Bugs Moran's crews in 1929. Not even a hint.

The man who called himself Strings reached into a pocket and pulled out a garrote consisting of a two foot long length of piano wire with a piece of wood on each end. "One of my strings," he explained. "I'm up to eighteen now. So that's the, what you call it, plurals, of string. Strings. I like doing my work close and personal like."

"Okay," Ivar said, following his personal rule of never disagree with a man who just claimed to have murdered 18 people. By hand. With a garrote. "If Capone is out of town, why did I need the note?"

"I needed it," Strings said. "To make sure you is who you say you is."

It is 1929 A.D. The world's population is 2,070,000,000, ie 2 billion, seventy million; Mussolini signs the Lateran Treaty making Vatican City a sovereign state and then uses the positive press to adopt a more aggressive foreign policy of trying to rebuild the Roman Empire (it doesn't turn out well); the 1st Academy Awards are given out and Wings *wins Best Picture in an Oscar ceremony that lasts a total of 15 minutes, speeches and all; the French begin work building a Big Wall to stop the Germans, called the Maginot Line—it didn't work as the Germans would simply go around it via the Low Countries (details are important); the Graf Zeppelin flies around the world in 21 days; A Farewell to Arms is published; Stalin sends Trotsky into exile and consolidates his power—it's estimated that eventually his regime kills 50 million (non-wartime death) Russians; the Dow Jones peaks at 381.17 before crashing on Black Tuesday (a date Ivar had visited on a previous mission), which it will not reach again until 1954, as 1929 turns out to be one of the worst years in recorded history; aka the worst of times.*

"You good with that piece you're packing?" Strings indicated the .45 semi-automatic in Ivar's shoulder holster.

"I can shoot," Ivar hedged.

"How about a Chicago typewriter?"

"A what?" But the download was faster. "A Thompson submachine gun?"

"Yeah. A tommy-gun." To make sure Ivar understood, Strings mimicked firing one. "Rat-a-tat-tat-tat."

"I've fired one," Ivar said, "but I'm not proficient."

Some things change; some don't.

"Okay, fair enough," Strings said. "Not like Tony or Sam is gonna give up their blaster anyways."

That clicked in the history of what was going to happen shortly. Two shooters with Thompson submachine guns would perpetrate the massacre. There was also supposed to be two gangsters dressed as cops to provide cover and deceive the victims into thinking it was just the usual shakedown. Four killers. Seven victims. Did that mean he and Strings were going to dress as cops?

"Where are the others?" Ivar asked.

"Around." Strings nodded toward a phone hanging on the wall. "We'll call them when the time is right." He indicated the building across the street and to the right: *SMC Cartage.*

Ivar slumped back in the booth, relieved he wasn't on the receiving end of the massacre that would shortly occur in that garage. "Can I get breakfast first?"

"Sure. Then we deliver a bloody Valentine."

"The only thing we have to fear is fear itself." Franklin Roosevelt

The Great Bitter Lake, 14 February 1945 A.D.

Eagle felt a trickle of sweat meander down his back. It was hot in the passageway on board the battle cruiser *USS Quincy.* But it was more than just the heat.

General Watson, President Franklin D. Roosevelt's Chief of Staff, spoke in a low, tired voice. "I imagine things are different where you're from. I guess I should say *when* you're from.

Still, even now, Negroes are serving with distinction on all fronts. It is to be expected that will continue and expand. I don't suppose you want to tell me when you are from?"

It is 1945 A.D.. Adolf Hitler takes up residence in the Fuhererbunker in Berlin on the 16th of January and will remain there until his death; Charles DeGaulle becomes President of France; Russians liberate the Lodz Ghetto—only 877 of the original 164,000 Jews who lived there are still alive; the world's first general purpose electronic computer, the ENIAC, is completed; Franklin D. Roosevelt is sworn in for a fourth term as President. And dies later that year.

"I can't," Eagle replied.

Some things change; some don't.

"Yes," Watson said. "The rules. Always rules. But rules are important. You know Franklin has a rule. He can't be photographed in the chair. So I have to help him up. Either me or his son, but James is in the Marines now." Once more his gaze grew vacant. "The President bears such a heavy burden. I wonder who will help him if I can't."

"Why do you say that?" Eagle asked, even though he knew the answer.

"I'm ill, son. You can see that. So is Franklin. I don't think either of us has much longer. I just hope I can last long enough to keep the President standing when he needs to. Because the country is going to need him to stand. Especially once he uses that A-bomb if those fellows in Los Alamos ever get the damn thing working. Oppenheimer says there will be nothing left of Berlin but ash. But I suppose you know the answer to how that turns out."

"Do just once what others say you can't do, and you will never pay attention to their limitations again." Captain James Cook

Hawaii, 14 February 1779 A.D.

A noise to one side along the beach alerted Roland. He turned, raising his weapons. A beautiful woman was walking toward him in the moonlight. She wore only a grass skirt, her perfect breasts aimed directly at Roland.

The Time Patrol's toughest soldier took a step back and looked from side to side, searching for an escape. He was on a rocky beach, waves crashing in on the right. Jungle to the left, ascending to a ridge. Danger to the front.

The woman was smiling. She stopped, gesturing with a hand for him to come to her.

Roland closed his eyes. "Neeley," he whispered, trying to get oriented.

It is 1779 A.D. The world's population is approaching 1 billion, but isn't quite there yet; the War of Bavarian Succession ends; Spain declares war on Britain in support of the American Revolution; Fort Nashborough, later to be known as Nashville, is founded on Christmas day; the British capture Savannah; John Paul Jones says he has not yet begun to fight, then fights harder and captures the HMS Serapis *while his own ship, the* Bonhomme Richard, *sinks. The American Revolution is in its fourth year and still has another four to go.*

When Roland opened his eyes, the half-naked woman was still there.

Some things change; some don't.

Roland shook his head. "No, thanks."

But he had a moment of doubt, not lust. Was this woman the mission? He wasn't renowned on the team for having much imagination, but he could hear Neeley's opinion on that as if she were standing next to him: *you wish*. She'd say it with humor, but Neeley's humor had to be taken seriously.

He spun about as he heard voices behind him, but it was just another sailor, dashing after a native girl who was laughing. They ran past without acknowledging Roland and disappeared into the darkness down the beach.

The woman gestured again and said something in a language Roland didn't understand and Edith hadn't bothered to download into his brain for the mission. But even Roland understood the implicit invitation in the tone and the way she stood.

He shook his head once more. "I've got a woman." He blushed, although it passed unseen. Calling Neeley his woman wasn't quite right.

The situation was exacerbated when a second, similarly undressed, woman came out of the jungle and joined the first. They both gestured for him to go with them into the jungle.

"Who are you?" Roland demanded.

The women looked at each other, then approached.

Roland took a step back. "Uh-uh."

He was still trying to figure out a way to escape this female ambush, when one of the women spoke in perfect English: "You are an odd man, Roland."

"The Dresden atrocity, tremendously expensive and meticulously planned, was so meaningless, finally, that only one person on the entire planet got any benefit from it. I am that person. I wrote this book, which earned a lot of money for me and made my reputation, such as it is. One way or another, I got two or three dollars for every person killed. Some business I'm in." Kurt Vonnegut
reference the Dresden bombing and his book *Slaughterhouse Five*

Dresden, Germany, 14 February 1945 A.D.

It was fortunate for Doc that Kurt Vonnegut had been a prisoner since the Battle of the Bulge the previous December, because the future author was weak from his meager POW diet. Thus even Doc, not exactly the most imposing physical specimen, was able to control Vonnegut, pinning him to the floor of the slaughterhouse.

Nearby, someone was yelling in German.

Doc looked up. One of the guards was pointing his rifle at the two of them, gesturing for them to move toward a stairway that went to the lower levels. The flickering light from the target indicator flares in the night sky outside was a motivator to do as the guard was ordering.

"We have to get underground," Doc yelled at Vonnegut, letting go of him and struggling to his feet. "This whole city is going to be an inferno!"

It is 1945 A.D.. The world's population is roughly 2,300,000,000 ie 2 billion, 300 million, although World War II is tinkering with that number; not in a good way. Over 60 million people are estimated to die in this war, roughly three percent of the entire human species, although some estimates bump that number to 80 million when including famine and war-related diseases. The Soviet Union suffers the most, with 13.7% of its population dying. Interestingly, Greece is next with somewhere between 7 to 11 percent of its population among the dead, while Nazi Germany suffers 8.26 to 8.86% loss. The United States suffers 407,300 combat deaths, equating to .32% of its population with only six people killed in an attack on American soil when a woman and five children stumble across a Japanese balloon bomb in Oregon.

A four thousand pound blockbuster bomb thundered nearby and the building shook.

Some things change; some don't.

A guard was behind Vonnegut, unseen by the perhaps-future author. The guard raised his rifle in a way Doc had seen during training—to smash the butt of it into the back of Vonnegut's skull stopping any book from ever being written.

Doc rushed forward, shoving Vonnegut aside.

The last thing he saw was the butt of the rifle coming for his own head.

And then darkness fell.

'Wanted: Women With Degrees in Mathematics . . . Women are being offered scientific and engineering jobs where formerly men were preferred. Now is the time to consider your job in science and engineering... You will find that the slogan there as elsewhere is 'WOMEN WANTED!' Recruitment ad for ENIAC, 1945.

Philadelphia PA, 14 February 1946

Moms leaned forward and listened to the women. One of them threw a Ping-Pong ball across the room containing the ENIAC computer. "If this is all he thinks we're good for, I say we quit." The ball bounced against one of the computer consoles.

"I agree," one of the others said. "We keep talking and talking, but we have to make a stand."

The other four women had big knives and were slicing Ping-Pong balls, painted either red or green, in half.

"You can keep yapping or you can help," one of the slicers said. "Sooner we get this done, the sooner we get out of here. We have to be back early in the morning to get ready for the press. I'd like to get some shut-eye."

"It is what it is," another slicer said. "Nothing's changed and nothing is going to change."

Was this just about stopping the women from quitting? Moms wondered. The prototype ENIAC computer was going to be publicly displayed tomorrow for the first time, so they'd already done the important work. The download informed her that these women, the ENIAC Six, were still needed after that. They were the only ones who could program it and, as importantly, find and quickly repair one of the tens of thousands of vacuum tubes, which burnt out on a regular basis.

It is 1946. Women vote for the first time in Italy as it turns from a monarchy into a Republic; the Philippines become independent after western control for 380 years; the bikini is first modeled on a runway in Paris; with no direct connection, Bikini Atoll is blasted by a series of nuclear tests; Project Diana bounces radio waves off the moon, accurately measuring the distance and also proving that communication is possible in outer space; Trygve Lie of Norway becomes the first United Nations Secretary-General; an explosion kills 400 coal miners in West

Germany; Ho Chi Minh becomes President of North Vietnam; Juan Peron becomes President of Argentina; an earthquake in Alaska initiates a tsunami which eventually hits Hawaii, killing roughly 170; It's A Wonderful Life *premieres.*

The mystery of the sliced Ping-Pong balls was solved when one of the women took several halves to a machine and glued a piece over one of the lights, changing it from a simple indicator to something that appeared more, well, technical?

Some things change; some don't.

"Just like those blinking lights in those terrible science fiction movies," the woman said, holding the piece in place, letting the glue dry. "Which of those brainiacs thought of this?"

"Someone in public affairs," another said. "Dog and pony show."

"Which are we?" another asked.

Moms wondered: Why was she *here*? *Now*?

Scout had run a mission in 1969 involving the development of computing—the day the first Internet message had been sent on Black Tuesday. The Shadow had tried to stop that with a bomb. Moms checked the download, going over the schematic of the building. She grimaced as she remembered all the explosives classes Mac had taught the team at the Ranch outside Area 51. He'd explained how to emplace them in order to do the most damage. Mac was gone now, disappeared on the D-Day, 1944 mission. A troubled man, she hoped he had found some peace before his end, whatever that had been in the echoing vastness of the past.

Moms walked to the stairwell and went to check the room above the main computer lab. A great place to emplace a shaped charge designed to explode downward, taking out whoever was in the room and the equipment.

She pushed open a door, entering a room with the same dimensions as the lab below. It was full of discarded tables, desks, chairs, filing cabinets and other school debris. It was dim, just a few naked light bulbs casting shadows among the furniture. Moms wove her way through, checking left and right.

She wasn't overly surprised when she saw the bomb, a large steel cylinder, emplaced between two desks.

What was most worrisome was the red digital countdown.

It read *:30* and as she watched, flickered to *:29*.

"There sat a queen who was more lovely by far than any other creature, just as the summer sun outshines the stars. This noble goddess Nature sat enthroned in a pavilion she had wrought of branches upon a flowered hill atop a meadow. And there was not any bird born of love that was not ready in her presence to hear her and receive her judgment. For this was Saint Valentine's Day, when all the birds of every kind that men can imagine come to choose their mates."

Chaucer: Parliament of Fowls

Italy, 14 February 278 A.D.

Scout recognized the voice behind her. "What do you want?"

"Is that any way to say hello to an old friend?" Pandora asked. "We last met, let me think, ah yes, in Greece. I forget the year."

"I doubt that," Scout said, turning away from the Tiber River to face the 'goddess'.

"Three-sixty-two BC," Pandora said, "or the more politically correct BCE."

Scout took a step toward her. "See? Why try to BS me?"

Pandora laughed. "Touché. Nice. But the important question isn't what I want, it's why are you here? Now? That's what I meant when I said that you're early. This place isn't important for another thirty-four years and in October."

Edith's download supplied the answer: The Battle of Milvian Bridge on 28 October 312.

"This is where and when the bubble is," Scout said. "What are you doing here?"

"Trying to understand what is going on," Pandora said. "Why do you think you're here?"

"Saint Valentine," Scout said.

"You shouldn't be here and now," Pandora said.

It is 278 A.D. The world's population is 300 million people; life expectancy is under 30 years; Emperor Probus resettles Germanic tribes in provinces of the Roman Empire to repopulate them which is rather short-sighted given what will eventually happen; Yang Hu, general of Jin Dynasty, dies; Christianity is still being persecuted in the Roman Empire and elsewhere, although the battle that would occur here in several decades would help change that.

Scout hated circular logic. "It's a Shadow bubble. It's opening bubbles on other Fourteen Februaries. This is mine."

Some things change; some don't.

Scout began to walk by Pandora to scramble up to the roadway to see what was happening on the bridge above them, but Pandora put a hand out.

"This is wrong. You being here. Now. That's why I'm here. Saint Valentine? How could that cause a ripple, never mind a Cascade? There were several Valentines; even the Church named four. The date is a myth coalesced through literature a millennium later."

Scout had begun to push against Pandora's arm, but she stopped. "So why am I here?"

"I can only deduce it's because the Shadow wants you here."

But *Before* Valentines Day, and *After* They Came Back From Nine Eleven

The Possibility Palace
Where? Can't tell you. When? Can't tell you.

LARA: *I'm in a dream, but the problem is my dreams are not much different than my reality. I can get hurt in them. I can get killed.*

At least I think so. On that dead thing, since I'm not dead yet.

Not Dead Yet. Monty Python.

Where did that come from? Who is Monty Python?

But I have been hurt in my dreams. That I am certain of. As far as dead, there's a first for everything.

And a last.

I'm in the same kitchen. The one I thought I'd left behind. The one I never like visiting.

But there is no man in here this time. No knife dripping blood. No blood trail leading through the door to a slaughtered family in the next room.

This seems to be an improvement.

But I still don't want to go through that door. Because while I know there is no dead family on the other side, there is something much worse than a slaughtered younger sister, a younger brother, a mother and a father.

I know that as much as I know anything, which means a lot and also not much. I know that to see what is really there, in my own past before that which I can remember, is so much worse than the nightmare.

I don't want to see.

But something is pushing me to see. Something I can't fight.

I take a step I can't control toward the door.

I'd really like to wake up. That's always the weird thing about my dreams, especially the nightmares. I know sometimes that I'm asleep. Really know it. Seems like if you know that, are conscious of it, then you should be able to reach consciousness, right?

But I can't.

Isn't that the worst feeling in the world?

I take another step.

I really don't want to see what's on the other side of that door. Because worse than dead family?

Really?

I'm aware that in reality I'm lying on a decent mattress covered by a cheap sheet. Not as bad as the one in the Fifth Floor cell, but still not a high thread count. Not bad, just not good. Something acquired in bulk with lots of other sheets and washed in large machines.

I focus on that. A big washing machine spinning, spinning.

A big pit. I can see it. Massive. That orients me to where my body is.

I'm in the Possibility Palace. Close to the Pit. I can sense the presence of that massive spiral of history not far away.

I'm in the team bunkroom.

That's good.

But I still take another step in the dream.

That's bad.

I hear a door open. Outside of the dream. In the reality I can't get to.

A threat?

A dream-line?

An enemy?

The intruder doesn't say anything. I hate that, but it let's me know who. One-Eye. The shrink who helps no one.

"I know there's more to you than you're telling us."

The words, real words, are a dream-line to reality. I can grab onto it, but do I want to touch it? Coming from this guy? That can't be good.

But worse than what's on the other side of that door?

"How did you get on that Russian plane?"

Good question. And the question is strengthening the line from the reality outside of my nightmare and keeps me from taking another dream step. So something.

"Open your eyes. I know you're not sleeping. I can see your pulse. Your temperature. You people might have your 'Sight' but I've got mine."

I'd really like to buddy, but I can't on your dream-line. It stinks. It's rotten. Fetid, like you are.

Where the hell did I learn the word 'fetid'?

Where is Moms? She'd get him out of here and get me out of this nightmare.

The door in the dream is beginning to open. But I'm not touching it. Who is opening it?

I really don't want to know.

I don't want to see beyond.

"What the frak?"

Scout. I grab for her voice, her dream-line.

"What are you doing in here?" Scout demanded.

"My job," Frasier replied.

"Are you some kind of creep? Watching a sleeping girl?"

"She's not asleep."

"Lara."

I work my eyelids, but they're so heavy. Made of steel, welded shut.

A hand on my shoulder. Gentle. Powerful. Love. The welding melts.

"Lara?"

My eyelids are heavy shutters, slowly rolling open.

"You okay?" Scout was leaning over Lara, her short, bright red hair a welcome sight.

"Bad dream," Lara muttered, blinking, focusing.

"Nightmare?" Scout asked.

"Yeah."

"Hate them," Scout said. She didn't look away, but addressed Frasier. "You can leave now."

"It wasn't dreaming," Frasier said. "It was something else. She wasn't asleep."

"You know this how?" Scout asked.

Frasier pointed to his solid black eyeball. "I see things that others don't see. Just like you."

"Not like me," Scout said.

"Her body temperature was below normal," Frasier said. "Her brain was even colder than her body. At a temperature where she should suffer damage. But she doesn't. And her pulse was much too fast for sleep. She's been like that before. It's not sleep. It's something else."

Scout gave Frasier her full attention, but kept her hand on Lara's shoulder. "You don't want to know what *I* see right now."

Lara shivered, feeling something roiling off Scout, dark and foreboding.

Not love.

Frasier took two involuntary steps back, his hand fumbling for the door. "I'm here on Dane's orders."

"His specific order?" Scout moved toward him. "He told you to sneak in here? Into our team room?"

"He ordered me to find out the truth about her." Frasier pointed toward Lara.

"She's part of the Team," Scout said. "That's the only truth you need to know. Be gone now."

And Frasier did leave, scurrying out the door.

"Whoa," Lara said. "You made him do that."

"I don't know if I did," Scout said. "But I wanted him out of here."

"I felt it," Lara said. "Power." She got off the bed. "That guy freaks me out."

"He freaks everyone out," Scout said. "Sounds like you and I have a similar problem."

"What's that?" Lara asked as she headed over to the fridge, and retrieved a tub of ice cream. She held it up, eyebrow arcing in question.

Scout nodded. "Where'd that come from?"

"I asked for it," Lara said.

Scout laughed. "Okay."

"So what's our similar problem?" Lara said.

"We're not sure where we come from. I thought I knew who my mother and father were. Turns out they weren't my parents. Which is actually kind of a relief, since they were sort of losers. Not like they hung me in a closet and beat me with a broomstick, but they were kind of nothings."

Lara brought the ice cream over, along with two spoons. "I thought I had a mother and father too. I was wrong about that. Which was a relief in a different way. The father I thought I had was a son-of-a-bitch. My mother I thought I had was weak. Worse than a nothing when you're with a bad something."

Scout went over to her bunk and sat down. Lara settled in next to her. Both were approaching the end of their teen years, although Scout was older. While Scout's short hair was bright red, Lara had a slight dark fuzz beginning to cover the scars on her scalp.

They sat in silence for a long time, each occasionally dipping into the melting ice cream.

*****

"Where is Dominic?" Ivar demanded.

"That's what we'd like to know," Dane said.

The two were in Foreman's office. Square, painted bland off-white, the only furniture an old wooden table with some chairs. There were a couple of folders and several scrolls on the top of the table, within Dane's reach. Ivar was seated across from him. The rest of the members of the team had scattered after being debriefed from their Nine-Eleven mission, except for Scout and Lara who were in the team room. But Ivar had something important on his mind.

"I handed him to Foreman in 1973," Ivar said. "What was Foreman doing in Chile?"

They were in the Possibility Palace, the headquarters of the Time Patrol. The room was off the spiral ramp that went around the massive Pit that descended into all of recorded history, where Analysts on the ramp worked constantly, tracking history, looking for any aberrations in the timeline.

Where and when the Possibility Palace existed was the most closely guarded secret of the Patrol. The Agents, who faced operatives of the Shadow on their missions, certainly didn't have a need to know.

"Obviously, Foreman was there to take Dominic," Dane said. He was the Administrator of the Patrol, a refugee from an Earth timeline destroyed by the Shadow. In his late seventies, his hair was shorn tight to his skull, getting greyer by the day, and his face lined with worry. He had over fifty years on Ivar, a former graduate student who'd 'joined' the Nightstalkers during the *Fun in North Carolina*, where the team had shut a rift in time-space.

When the Nightstalkers became the Time Patrol, Ivar had sensed he had little option but to go along, although, like all team members, he'd been given a choice by Dane: move forward or go back to one specific moment in his life and change something.

After all, one could not be a member of the Time Patrol if one had an inclination to change the past.

In his darker moments, of which there were many, Ivar wondered if the choice were real or a use, where it was actually *join or disappear*?

"I mean," Ivar clarified, "where is Dominic *now*? Is he still alive? When I was traveling back, I sensed he became one of the Missing in Chile. One of those who simply disappeared after the coup. Did Foreman turn him over to the junta?"

Dane shook his head. "He didn't go missing." They were discussing the young boy Ivar had rescued in the midst of that coup back on 11 September 1973. "Foreman brought him to us not long after that. Here."

Ivar was surprised. "Then he's here now?"

Ivar was a thin, young man with shaggy dark hair. He'd always appeared nervous, uncertain, but after several Time Patrol missions, especially his first when he'd been dumped into Long Island Sound wearing cement overshoes by Meyer Lansky, he'd begun changing. Maturing? Growing harder; more cynical? It was difficult to tell. There was also the issue of having been replicated by whatever had been on the other side of that Rift in North Carolina several times, to the point where he'd wondered if he were the original Ivar; although a Fate had assured him he was; as if that were assurance to be told by some being whose very essence was a mystery?

"He's no longer here." Dane sighed. "Dominic *was* here for many years. A most singular young man. But during the Nine-Eleven mission something happened."

"'Something'?"

"He disappeared."

"To where?" Ivar demanded.

"We don't know." Dane sighed. "He snapped out of existence. Perhaps the result of a ripple from your mission."

"He was fine when I gave him to Foreman," Ivar said.

"I'm sure he was. But that was decades ago in real time."

"How could my mission have made him disappear when my mission actually got him here in the first place?"

"We don't know if it did make him disappear," Dane answered. "But it might have closed a loop from outside our timeline, since he came from outside of it."

"What did Dominic do here?"

"He tried to see the future," Dane said.

Ivar wasn't surprised given what he'd experienced with Dominic and his mother during the mission to Chile. "Did he?"

"We look to the past, Ivar. We keep it intact. The future is only possibilities. It doesn't exist yet. Not like the past. Time travel only works one way. We can't travel, or see, into a future that hasn't occurred yet.

"Dominic had the Sight," Dane continued. "The most we'd ever seen in a man. He lived here, in his own place. He read reports from the analysts. Twice he wrote something down on a scroll. A vision of what he believed to be the future. Once in 2001. And once during the Nine Eleven mission. But it appears there was nothing. The most recent scroll was blank when it was opened by Hannah at the Cellar, to whom he insisted it be delivered."

"Was that before or after he disappeared?" Ivar asked.

"We're not certain," Dane said.

"What about the prediction in 2001?"

Dane shrugged. "We don't know. The man who opened it is dead."

"Odd choice of years to have a vision. Was *that* before Nine-Eleven?"

"It was."

"Did his vision have something to do with that? With our Nine-Eleven missions?"

"We don't know. If there was anything on it, it's dead with Hannah's predecessor. The predictions, like Dominic, might have been loops that disappeared when he did."

"So what happened to Dominic?" Ivar pressed. "Where did he disappear to?"

"Where does anyone disappear to?" Dane replied. "He's gone, as if he were never here."

"Did he go through a Gate? To the Space Between?"

Dane looked down at the table top. "No. He was with Lara. She says he was there, then he wasn't."

"The way we appear in a Shadow bubble," Ivar said. "We're not there, then we're there. Except he was here, then not here."

"It appears so," Dane said. "Lara couldn't explain it."

"So Dominic was an anomaly in time. Just like Rasputin during Doc's Tsar mission. I've been thinking about it. If Rasputin was influenced by Valkyries and acting for the Shadow then he *did* change our history and we didn't correct that. There have been other events during our missions where—"

Dane cut him off. "Hold on. History is what it is. Our mission is to maintain it. Rasputin did live. He did influence the Tsarina. Doc's job on his Ides mission wasn't Rasputin. It was to insure Tsar Nicholas abdicated. He stopped the Tsarina's plan to change her husband's decision. That's all there is to that. Don't overthink this."

"Just do as I'm ordered?"

"You can always resign," Dane said.

"And have Hannah send someone from the Cellar to visit me?" Ivar asked. "Perhaps Roland's girlfriend, Neeley? Hell, Roland would do me in himself if you told him to. Not too many original ideas in his head. The two of them could make it a play date, then go have lunch."

"You could work for us in the present," Dane said. "Continue your research into the Turing Time Computer. Try to discern what the Shadow's plan is. Maybe even figure out where they'll strike next *before* they start to open their bubble."

"Wouldn't that be looking into the future?"

"It would be giving us intelligence on possibilities," Dane said.

Ivar leaned back in the hard wooden chair. "I've never been a part of," he finally said.

Dane waited.

"This team is all I have," Ivar said. "The closest I've got to family. You know I have no one back in the present; assuming we're not in the present here and I seriously doubt that we are. If I'd had any strong ties I wouldn't have been asked to join. No one on the team has anyone back there in the world. Hell, Mrs. Jones would've never brought me into the Nightstalkers if she hadn't been sure I'd sign on. I don't think many people said no to her." He stood. "I'm here to stay. I'll go on missions. I'll work on the Turing when I'm here in the Palace or back in our time. But I don't think we know all we think we know. I don't think you know all. There's more to all this. And I'm keeping my eyes open for it."

"An open mind is fine," Dane said, "as long as you adhere to the rules of the Time Patrol."

Ivar leaned forward, putting his hands on the table. "Let me ask you something. We've been on the run ever since we got recruited. But there's something that's been bugging me. That no one else has brought up. Maybe they've blocked it out. Maybe it doesn't matter. But when the Nightstalkers were initially alerted, we were told we were looking for the Time Patrol. The team before us. But then, once we took out the Ratnik, we were told that it was just a recruitment test. But there *was* another team before us, wasn't there? There had to be. This place just wasn't sitting here, waiting for us to show up."

Dane didn't respond.

"And you're not going to tell me what happened to the team before us, are you?"

"You don't have a need to know," Dane said. "Do you have any plans for your time off?"

"Are you asking if I'm going to Chile?" Ivar asked. "Visit where I did my last mission, like the others do?"

"I was being friendly," Dane said, which elicited a look of disbelief from Ivar.

"No point in going to Chile," Ivar said, "if Foreman brought Dominic here. There's nothing there for me. I'm going to meet up with Doc in New York City. I've got a theory that might help with the Turing Time Computer I need to discuss with him."

Dane raised an eyebrow. "What is that?"

"Math."

Nine-Eleven Memorial, New York City.

It is never easy to commemorate the dead. Over his years of service, Eagle had attended numerous ceremonies and conducted eulogies for fallen comrades. Too many.

He'd carved names into the table in the Den while the team was the Nightstalkers and had added names to the table in their Time Patrol team room inside the Possibility Palace.

The solemn aura of this place was palpable, seven stories below Manhattan street level. People spoke in hushed whispers. No one was taking selfies.

Eagle stood in front of a wall covered with 2,983 individual paper watercolors in different shades of blue. Each one paid tribute to a person who'd died on 9-11 or in the 1993 Trade Center bombing.

Beyond the wall was the private repository of over 8,000 human remains.

Inscribed on the wall were letters forged in steel recovered from the wreckage of the World Trade Center. The letters were fifteen inches tall and highlighted by subtle spotlights.

Eagle read the quote once more, processing the words:

No Day Shall Erase You From the Memory of Time

Virgil

Eagle, who's been recruited into the Nightstalkers not only because of his superb skills as a pilot and soldier, but also for his prodigious memory, knew exactly where the quote came from. Book IX of the *Aeneid* by Virgil. He was shaking his head.

"I know." Standing next to Eagle was Edith Frobish, the team's art historian and finder of artifacts. While her memory wasn't as extensive as his, her advanced education and occupation, working ostensibly as a historian in the Metropolitan Museum of Art, allowed her to converse on a relatively level intellectual playing field with him. "Not quite right."

"Quite wrong," Eagle said, "if taken in context of the original text."

"Two Trojan soldiers, correct?" Edith asked.

"Nisus and Euryalus," Eagle said. "They're with Aeneas, fleeing Troy after it was sacked. They go to Italy. To found what would become Rome. At least that's the story inside the story. Their camp is surrounded by enemies, so the two venture out in the dark and kill enemy soldiers while they're sleeping. They're captured in the midst of doing this terrible deed, their heads are cut off, and then paraded in front of the Trojan camp. Why would someone think that appropriate for the innocents who died on Nine-Eleven?"

"Most people don't know the context," Edith pointed out. "Standing by itself, it resonates."

"I suppose."

"Sometimes you have to just look at the microcosm, not the entire system," Edith said. "This entire place was initiated by tragedy. And then grew amidst controversy. There was no way to please everyone. This is all a compromise in the face of great emotion."

"True," Eagle agreed. "But perhaps something along the lines of Kipling's lifting from the 44th chapter of Ecclesiastics for the World War I Memorial would have been better. It's not about soldiers but about those who die having performed great deeds but also obscurely, whose names might not be remembered by history, but will be by their family and friends. '*Their seed shall remain forever, and their glory shall not be blotted out. Their bodies are buried in peace; but their name liveth for evermore*'."

"Is that how you feel?" Edith asked.

Eagle raised an eyebrow in question. Off to their left was the remains of the antennae that had once stood so far above the ground on top of the North Tower; now a mangled mass of steel and wires.

Edith gave a quick glance about to make sure no one was in earshot. "About the Time Patrol? About battling in secrecy but carving their names in the team room? Reciting their true names? No one but the Team knows of their sacrifice?"

"Sometimes," Eagle allowed. The ebony skin on the left side of his shaved skull was pockmarked and rippled from an IED explosion suffered in a war that no longer seemed significant, yet still dragged on. He was six feet tall and carried himself with that unique aura that those in elite units simply had.

Edith matched him in height, with a lean dancer's body and a prominent, sharp nose. She held a special place in the Time Patrol because it had been learned that one of the greatest recorders of history is art. If the art changes, then history has changed. While the analysts in the Pit toiled away, Edith was in the here and now, headquarters the Met, always checking on the status of art.

"What I don't get," Eagle said, "is why we couldn't stop this." In his own time sense, he was just days removed from 9-11-2001, and was uncertain whether what he felt came from this hallowed ground or his recent experience, or a confusing mixture of the two.

Edith frowned. "Your Nine-Eleven mission? It didn't have anything to do with what happened here in New York."

"I know." Eagle sighed. "Nothing good came from that terrible day. Not up to our present as far as I can tell. Just endless war and terrorism. Why didn't we stop it?"

"We don't know what the alternatives could have been," Edith said. "I'm sure there's at least one timeline where Nine Eleven, as we know it, didn't happen. But we don't know if the variables might have been worse."

"We don't know if it might have been better, either," Eagle said.

"We're here," Edith said, reverting to the standard justification of the Time Patrol; not one said lightly given all the timelines that no longer existed. "And you stopped the Shadow from getting Tsar Bomba. Who knows what it would have done with that horrible weapon?"

"I checked," Eagle said. "There's no sign of the wreckage of the Shadow Sphere in the Barents Sea. That thing was huge."

"Objects out of their timeline collapse when the time bubble implodes," Edith said. "There shouldn't be any sign." She put an arm around his shoulder. "The important thing is *you're* here."

They remained still, each deep in thought for a little while before Eagle spoke again. "It's all so strange," he said. "I don't feel like I belong here."

"The place or time?" Edith asked.

"Both."

Edith indicated the stairs. "Do you want to leave?"

Eagle nodded.

Hand-in-hand they headed for the exit, but then Eagle's satphone rang, the ringtone familiar: Warren Zevon's *Send Lawyers Guns and Money*.

Fort Meade, Maryland

Roland had survived numerous ambushes on his various deployments overseas in the Army and his missions in the Nightstalkers and Time Patrol. But as he watched the two women approaching, he was at a loss how to react. Correct procedure, drummed into Roland's particularly thick skull during Ranger School years ago, was to assault directly into the ambush.

Attack the attackers.

Except one of them was Neeley and he could no more 'attack' her in any form as run away. A lose-lose scenario. So he stood his ground and braced himself for the unexpected.

He was standing outside the 'Puzzle Palace', the headquarters of the National Security Agency, located on Fort Meade, but separated from the rest of the military installation, surrounded by its own intense cordon of security. The building that the two women were coming out of was covered in one-way black glass which was lined with copper shielding to prevent any unwanted signals or sounds to come in, or, more importantly, out.

Roland's I.D. had the highest security clearance possible, but he still sensed eyes on him, both electronic—to be assumed here—and also human. This was one of the most secure places on the planet, but Roland came from a place, the Possibility Palace, that those inside of the Puzzle Palace had no clue existed.

"Roland," Neeley said, as the two reached him, "this is Hannah Masterson, my boss. And friend. Hannah, this is my Roland."

Roland flushed, not at meeting a woman he'd heard dark stories about, but because Neeley had said 'my'. He studied the other woman with the frank assessment of a man who viewed everyone as a potential adversary first, possible ally next, or, usually, someone to be disregarded.

Hannah was over a foot shorter than Roland's six and a half. Her thick hair had been darkened; Roland now knew about the importance of that after Scout had berated him for not noticing Neeley's recent attempt to become more fashionable. There were deep worry lines etched around her dark brown eyes, to be expected of someone with her responsibilities. She was trim and appeared fit, something Roland noticed and judged in everyone.

"I had to meet you, Roland," Hannah said, extending her hand.

Roland took it, gingerly, as if touching a delicate vase, but was surprised at her firm grip. He realized anyone who ran the Cellar, the 'police' of the covert world, would have to be tough. He just hadn't expected her to be physically tough since she looked like the suburban housewife that she had, in fact, once been.

Neeley, on the other hand, resembled both her occupation, assassin, and someone who could hold her own with Roland. Six feet tall, wiry, short black hair, recently darkened, she projected no nonsense.

"Um, pleased to meet you," Roland said, his face flushing even darker.

"Neeley and I go back a while," Hannah said, "I'm not sure what she's told you of our past."

Roland didn't think that was a question, because if it was, it was part of the ambush, so he shuffled his feet and said nothing.

"Hannah, be nice," Neeley said. "Roland's clearance is higher than mine."

Hannah smiled, but even Roland could feel the lack of warmth. She was assessing him in the same manner he had done her, but with a depth that disconcerted Roland.

"You and Neeley have worked well together," Hannah said.

"Yes, ma'am," Roland said.

A twitch on the edge of Hanna's mouth; amusement. "That's one letter from Madam. I don't run a whorehouse, Roland. You can call me Hannah."

"Yes, ma'—" Roland began, but caught himself. "All right. Hannah."

The three stood awkwardly and then Roland was rescued by a call to action as his phone chimed with *Send Lawyers Guns and Money*.

"They'll wonder where that call came from," Hannah said, indicating the black-glass building. "Someone in there is trying to figure that out and getting very frustrated. The NSA doesn't like being frustrated. Of course, they wonder where I come from even though my office is under their building. And I wonder where you come from, so it's quite the puzzle, wrapped in an enigma." She suddenly changed, reaching out and putting a hand on Roland's well-muscled forearm as he pulled the satphone out to answer with his other hand. "You take care of yourself, Roland. You're important to Neeley and she's my friend."

Roland wasn't sure if that was a kind gesture or a threat. And he noted that she didn't say take care of Neeley—the implication, of course, that Neeley was more than capable of doing that.

The Billop House, Staten Island, New York

Nothing. Doc felt nothing. No ghostly spirit flitting about, no Fate hovering in the ethereal plane waiting to pass judgment, no mythical Goddess and her Pandora's box of ill.

Just cold as the wind whipped along the beach on the Staten Island side of Arthur Kill, the narrow waterway separating it from New Jersey. It also smelled pretty bad, since he was across from the swamps of northern New Jersey and surrounded by the various refineries dotting the shoreline on both sides. He was at the southwest corner of Staten Island.

Doc turned away from the water and looked at the old Billop House. He reached in a pocket and retrieved a pair of old spectacles. Very old. Doc turned them over, knowing he should have reported them during debrief after the Nine-Eleven mission, but a part of him felt that they were his; earned by saving Benjamin Franklin's life from the Legion assassin.

Technically, of course, Doc knew he'd had help. Pandora and Pyrrha.

And the ghost of Billop House, a young serving girl murdered by the original owner.

At least the girl was at peace now.

Doc walked toward the old house, now in the National Register of Historic Places. Here, on 11 September 1776, Benjamin Franklin, John Adams and Edward Rutledge had met with Admiral Howe to negotiate a possible peace between the Colonies and the Crown.

The negotiations had failed.

That much Doc knew to be true.

He paused, went to one knee, and vomited.

He'd been assured he was healthy, despite the radiation he'd been bathed in during the D-Day mission in Pakistan. He'd been treated with cutting edge medicine, Atlantean medicine, he'd been told by Dane.

Was that true? He didn't feel healthy. Doc knew that the Russian Army used to issue its soldiers pills labeled 'anti-radiation'. A placebo to keep them fighting through a nuclear wasteland as long as they could.

Doc stood and continued toward the house. His parents had emigrated from India when he was young, desiring a better life for their offspring. His skin was dark and he wore thick glasses, an anathema on the Team. But the Time Patrol was more than just military. It, and the Nighstalkers they were before, battled on the edge of science and beyond.

Doc touched the side of the old house. It was real. But was his experience here real? One had to wonder or one would never wonder at anything.

Tsar Nicholas and the Tsarina? Anastasia peering at him through a window in the palace as he faced a firing a squad, only to escape at the last second by traveling back to his own time while she was trapped to face her fate? Pakistan and the nukes? Thomas Jefferson, Benjamin Franklin, John Adams and the Declaration of Independence *and* the never revealed Declaration of Emancipation? Then here, for a peace conference that accomplished nothing but could have stopped the Revolution, and the United States, in 1776?

Doc held up the spectacles. They felt real. The house was real to his touch.

He remembered the words. Pandora's word, why she'd kept *Elpis*, hope, in her pithos, denying it to mankind:

"Most hope is selfish. It is hope based on the way each person who is hoping envisions the future. Not the way the future should be for everyone, but for himself or herself. It is the cornerstone of many religions where people hope there is a heaven, thus focusing on the future. Hope is not grounded in the here and now. All we have is the here and now."

Doc had disagreed but he knew there was a kernel of truth in what she said. Mankind had a marvelous talent for fooling itself. The blindness of irrationality. Of selfishness. Of hoping for the self, not for the greater good.

He'd seen it in Russia in 1917; in Pakistan in 1998; Philadelphia in 1776 and later that same year here, where Benjamin Franklin and John Adams and Admiral Howe could have prevented the Revolutionary War if they'd had to the authority and the willingness.

And if Doc hadn't shown up to make sure that the peace negotiations came to nothing.

His musings were interrupted:

Send Lawyers Guns and Money

He heard a helicopter coming in fast and low. He smiled as Ivar slid open the side door and waved him in. Ivar handed him a headset and Doc put it on as he sat down.

"Dane send you to pick me up?" Doc asked.

Ivar shook his head. "Timing. I was just Zevoned while coming to join you."

The chopper lifted up and banked over Staten Island toward Manhattan and the Metropolitan Museum of Art, where the Gate to take them to the Possibility Palace was hidden deep beneath the surface.

"I've been thinking about something you told me," Ivar said.

"What was that?"

"That math is the quantification of reality."

"And?" Doc was shaken, as if Ivar had picked up his earlier thoughts.

"The Rule of Seven," Ivar said.

"What of it?"

"Why seven?" Ivar asked. "Why not six? Or eight?"

"That's the history," Doc said. "Atlantis was attacked by the Shadow for six straight years on the same day, and on the seventh, it was destroyed. The Shadow opens six bubbles on each day, trying to form Cascades that develop the seventh change, the tsunami. Seven has always been a significant number. Seven days in a week. On the seventh day, God rested. And so on."

"Math," Ivar said.

Doc didn't miss a beat. "Seven is a prime number. It's the only Mersenne safe prime number, actually, which is special."

"Indeed," Ivar said.

Doc was focused. "It's the lowest natural number that can't be represented as the sum of the square of three integers. And it is the most likely number to come up when rolling two dice." As they passed over the Manhattan shoreline and headed toward the Freedom Tower, he glanced over at Ivar. "Where are you going with this?"

"In catastrophe theory," Ivar said, "there are four possible catastrophes with one active variable and three with two variables. Seven possible types of catastrophes."

Doc was silent for a few moments. "Do you think the Shadow is trying to create each type of catastrophe somehow? We'd have to define the seven types and—"

"Single variable: fold, cusp, swallowtail, and butterfly. Double variable: hyperbolic, elliptic, and parabolic."

"—and then try to fit the changes the Shadow tried in each bubble to those," Doc finished.

"Yes," Ivar said.

Doc smiled. "If we return from this mission, it is something to explore."

"When we get back," Ivar corrected.

Doc wasn't looking at the Freedom Tower. He was staring at the footprint where the World Trade Center had once stood.

Mountain Meadows, Utah

The valley was more desolate than it had been over one hundred and fifty years ago. Over-grazing. Moms remembered that from the mission briefing. Edith Frobish had said something about it. Remembering Edith made Moms smile as she though of her with Eagle. Lots of brain-power there, but something more. Something good. Eagle needed something good.

Moms shivered, the cold wind blowing across the open land biting through her jacket.

Ghosts. All around. Moms could hear them. Mothers crying for their children. Men for their wives. Boys for their fathers.

There was only one other car in the parking lot. The site was on a north-south road in southwestern Utah that pretty much went from nowhere to nowhere. Well off today's beaten track but in 1857 it had been on one of the main westward wagon trails. The long valley had been a resting place before the final push across the Nevada deserts and then over the Sierras into the promised land of California.

For those of a certain wagon train in 1857, the promise had abruptly ended here.

A pile of stones inside an enclosure was the memorial for their deaths at the hands of Mormon militia.

"Did you have an ancestor here? When it happened?"

Moms was surprised she hadn't heard the old man coming up behind her. Roland would have been very upset with her, but Roland was on the east coast with Neeley and for a moment, Moms felt a pang of something she quickly ignored.

She had to consider how to answer the question. There were two sides here over one hundred and fifty years ago: the victims and their killers. "No," she lied. "Did you?"

"Yes." He was silent for a few moments, then spoke in a low voice. "*'I have been sacrificed in a cowardly, dastardly manner'.*"

"John D. Lee."

The old man gave a half nod. "You know the history. I'm a direct descendant. There're many of us. He had nineteen wives and fifty-six children." He gave a wry smile. "They don't talk about what happened here at family gatherings. Not at all." He pointed. "He was executed over there." He shifted his attention back to her. "Why do you know what he said just before they shot him?"

"I'm a student of history," Moms lied. She remembered Lee. The faces around the campfire as the awful decision was made by the Mormon militia to kill the emigrants in the wagon train. All of them, including women and children and even the babies. That was all she'd managed to avert, saving 17 very young lives, the way history recorded it

The old man seemed satisfied with that answer. "Anyone stopping here would have to be. Not many come here."

"Do you come here often?" Moms asked.

"I live here," he said. "Not here, *here*, but just a few miles away. Seems the past has drawn me with a power greater than my own. Ever feel that way?"

That truth wasn't hard. "Yes."

Moms phone chimed: *Lawyers, guns and money.*

"That's odd," the old man said. "There's no cell phone coverage."

"Special phone," Moms said, as she checked the screen to find out where she was getting picked up. She turned for her car in the parking lot.

The old man's voice gave her pause.

"I've wondered something," he said. "Something weird."

Moms turned. "What's that?"

The old man touched his chest. "I, my children, my grandchildren, all exist because John D. Lee lived. He wasn't executed until 1877, twenty years after the massacre. One of his sons was my direct ancestor and was born in those twenty years. There are probably close to a thousand people alive now because of him. So. My weird thought. If Lee had died before the massacre, or never existed, would the massacre never have happened? But I, and my family, wouldn't exist, right? So would I wish that, if wishing could make something true? Trade my existence, and my family, and all those other who are alive, for the people who died here?"

Moms felt the tug of the alert. Of mission. She remembered the voices around the campfire the night before the massacre and the arguments. "It doesn't matter. It would have happened anyway. It was inevitable given everything else. There were others responsible. He was the scapegoat. There would have been a different scapegoat, but those people would still be dead."

The old man nodded, but didn't look relieved in the slightest. "I imagine you're right."

The Possibility Palace
Where? Can't tell you. When? Can't tell you.

Dane looked like he was praying when Frasier, the Time Patrol psychiatrist, entered his office. Dane's hands were clasped together under his chin and his eyes were closed. There were six folders on the table in front of him, aligned perfectly.

"What did you find out about Lara?" Dane asked, without opening his eyes.

"I got alerted," Frasier said, indicating the folders, a wasted movement with most, but Frasier knew it wasn't. Not with Dane, who had some of the Sight.

"We'll get to that," Dane said. "It will take the team a little while to assemble and the bubble is still forming. There are a couple of anomalies in it I want to know more about."

"'Anomalies'?"

"Tell me about Lara."

Frasier sat down across from Dane. His left eye was a solid black orb, surrounded by scar tissue.

"She disappeared out of a black site eight months ago," Frasier said.

"Run by?"

"The CIA. They were using a mental institution as a front for experiments."

Dane opened his eyes. "LSD. Timothy Leary. Grill Flame. The Agency has been mucking about in that since they were founded. In a way they were more right than they knew, but in a way they were going in the wrong direction. The Sight is something that isn't easily quantifiable. Foreman always kept tabs on the CIA's experiments and research. How come he didn't know about Lara?"

Frasier held up his left hand, also a prosthetic. "The black site was obliterated at the time she disappeared so it was covered deep with concrete deniability. Every staffer and guard killed. She disappeared along with all records of her. I was only able to learn this by tracing secondary computer shadows at the Agency. They still haven't figured out what happened to the site. And they really thought she was a sixteen-year-old from Wichita who murdered her family. Father, mother, younger brother and sister."

"And she isn't?"

"She is," Frasier said. "But she isn't. There's no doubt the family was killed. And the girl, Lara Cole was her name, disappeared. But whether that Lara Cole is our Lara? Questionable. My conjecture is: doubtful, based on what I pieced together on the Wichita Lara Cole prior to the murders. It feels like someone appropriated her identity."

"What happened to the original Lara Cole?" Dane asked.

Frasier shrugged. "Gone."

"Did she kill her family?"

"I don't think so. More likely whoever took her, killed her family."

"So we still don't know who *our* Lara is," Dane summed up.

"No."

"Who attacked the black site?"

"Unknown."

"How did she end up with the Russians? And getting sent to us?"

"That's the strange thing," Frasier said. "Her Russian story? Fake."

"That can't be," Dane said. "The Russians confirmed they had her. They sent her."

"That's what they said and say," Frasier said. "But I did some digging and can't find anything to back up their story either."

"Sin Fen believed her story," Dane said, referring to the priestess who worked with the Time Patrol and had a large degree of the Sight.

Frasier spread his hands. "I can't vouch for what Sin Fen 'sees'. The only facts I can lock down are the CIA black site. And even that's sketchy. Checking the manifest for the Russian plane, they only sent two people. Not three."

"And yet," Dane didn't seem overly surprised, "three got off the plane. Where did it stop on the way over?"

Frasier shook his head. "It didn't. Direct with inflight refueling. They weren't taking any chances."

"And yet she was on board," Dane said. "And the guards didn't act like anything was amiss. And the Russians gave us a bunch of BS to back up her story. Interesting. She wasn't there and then she was there." He rubbed his forehead. "She's different. Very different. I don't think she's from this timeline. In fact, I very much doubt it."

Frasier didn't respond, because Dane wasn't from this timeline. The Dane of this timeline had died in Vietnam decades ago. Dane didn't speak of his timeline other than having said it didn't exist any more. Wiped out by the Shadow.

"And Lara now?"

"I think she goes places in that fugue state," Frasier said, choosing his words carefully. "In her mind. It looks like she's sleeping but she's not. She's somewhat aware of the world around her, but more focused on some place else. Or some other time. Her heart rate is high. The temperature drop in her body and especially her brain is especially intriguing. I can find nothing in the data banks like it."

"Any thoughts on it?"

"Perhaps a primal form of protection," Frasier suggested. "While her mind is gone, her body is minimizing energy expenditure. Hibernation."

"But you said her heart beat speeds up," Dane said.

"True," Frasier admitted. "I'm just speculating. Perhaps she went to Russia while she was in that state. A Russia in her mind? Or perhaps a Russia in a different timeline?"

"And you went into the team room again," Dane said.

"I did."

"I don't think you'll survive a third time."

Frasier took the rebuke as the order it was intended as. With no more questions forthcoming, he broke the silence. "What day?"

"Fourteen February."

Frasier frowned, which wrinkled the scar tissue around his machine eye in an unnatural way. "Valentines Day? Odd."

"Why odd?" Dane said. "One of three-hundred-and-sixty-five the Shadow has to choose from."

"Three-sixty-six, if we include leap years," Frasier said. "But nothing significant in history comes to mind for Fourteen February."

Dane put his hand on the folders. "Every day of the year has significant historical events. And even the insignificant can become significant over time. We have to remember the old adage *'for want of a nail, a shoe was lost'*."

Frasier indicated the table. "I don't have any folders."

"Your powers of observation are considerable."

Frasier waited. Dane opened the top folder and began reading. He wrote something on a sheet of paper paper-clipped to the cover. Then he opened the second one. He looked up. "Still here?"

The Mission Briefing

DOC WAS THE FIRST to enter the team room. He wore a faded leather bomber jacket that had seen better days and a bedraggled World War II Army Air Force flight suit with the elbows and knees worn thin. His new 'old' style glasses slid down on his nose and he pushed them back into place as he took a seat at the table.

He ran a hand along the worn leather of the other sleeve, wondering if this was a real relic from the time period or something that had been made here and aged in some way.

He started coughing, hard. He bent over trying to clear his throat, putting his hand over his mouth. It took a few moments, but then the spasm passed. He straightened and grabbed a chair, slumping into it. He looked up at the wall dotted with a few mementos from previous Time Patrol missions: an original Badge of Merit from George Washington, the forerunner of the Purple Heart; a gray-green scale from Aglaeca, the mother of Grendel, both very real monsters and much worse than the epic poem made them out to be.

Eagle came in, looking not too happy, which wasn't an unusual thing given the positions he often had to assume in order to travel into the past for his missions. He wore a white U.S. Navy uniform, from the same era as Doc's.

That was confirmed as Eagle checked out Doc's outfit. "Army Air Force. Before the Air Force became a separate branch. The shoulder patch is Eighth Air Force. Organized in early 1945 in Europe. So you're going toward the end of World War Two or just after."

"And yours?" Doc asked. "Navy, obviously."

"Same time frame," Eagle confirmed. "Except blacks, negroes as we were called then, on good days, weren't integrated in the services until 1948. So I'm serving as a cook or steward or some such crap." He sat down next to Doc. "I thought I *knew* history. A lot of it. But I didn't really *understand* some of it. Not my people's history in this country. What they went through."

Doc indicated his skin. "I have some empathy with you, my friend. Not quite the same, but similar."

Eagle nodded. "Yeah. I know. When people can tell you're not the same as them by your skin color, the world is a very different place."

"Would I fit in, in the Eighth Air Force?" Doc asked. "It was not easy being an obvious foreigner in 1776 in Philadelphia. I don't think Benjamin Franklin or John Adams bought into my lie."

"That was the least of your worries." Eagle indicated the Order of Military Merit on the wall. "Try being a slave in 1783 in George Washington's camp."

"But I am not a pilot, like you," Doc pointed out. "Will that not be a problem? Shouldn't you be wearing this?"

Eagle pointed at a metal pin on the breast of Doc's jacket. "Flight surgeon. That puts you in an interesting position in the unit. It was World War II. They were desperate for bodies. Eventually they even let negroes into combat units, although they had white officers. But a doctor? Even more valuable. Especially in a bomber unit."

"How so?"

"Ever read *Catch-22*?" Eagle asked. He didn't wait for an answer. "Only one in three airmen survived the war flying missions over Europe. The losses were staggering. And you're the man who can determine whether someone is on flight status or not. I think that's going to matter a lot more than your ethnic background."

Doc indicated the state of the jacket and the flight suit. "Not exactly straight from the laundry."

"True—" Eagle began but he paused. "You all right?"

"What do you mean?" Doc asked.

Eagle indicated a smear of blood on the arm of Doc's chair. "That yours'?"

Doc looked at his hand. "It's nothing."

"It's blood," Eagle said. "You cut yourself?"

Doc folded his hand into a fist. "Just a scratch."

Any further questioning was interrupted as the next member of the team came in.

Scout was dressed in an off-white robe, cinched at the waist with a rope. A step down in quality from what she'd worn on her missions to ancient Greece, a step up from being a beggar. "I just want to go to an era that has toilets," she said. "Is that too much to ask? Hot and cold running water? Showers? People smell better when there are showers. 1969 was nice. Why can't I go back to then?"

"Someone tried to kill you in 1969," Eagle pointed out.

"Two someones tried to kill me in 1969," Scout said. "Someone has tried to kill me every year I've gone back to. I want to die comfortable. And clean."

"Who's dying?" Ivar asked as he entered the Team Room.

"Looking good," Eagle said. "Better than any of us."

Ivar was dressed in a suit and carrying a fedora. He held aside the jacket so they could see the .45 caliber pistol in a leather shoulder holster. "At least I'm going strapped this time."

"Don't let Roland see it," Scout said, "or we'll get the history of the M1911A1 forty-five caliber pistol."

"You remembered your lessons from Fort Bragg," Eagle noted approvingly. "Roland would gladly point out the differences between the original M1911 and the A1 variation."

"The instructor was kinda persistent," Scout said. "I thought the important part was aiming and pulling the trigger, but no—" she didn't get to finish the history of her Special Ops training as the door from the prep area opened and Roland entered. They'd packed the big man into tight fitting white trousers which ended mid-calf, a calico shirt unbuttoned halfway to his waist, with a heavy cutlass stuck on one side in a leather belt at his side and a wicked looking axe in his hand.

Roland was excited. "I get to be a pirate!"

"Don't let Neeley see you in that," Scout said. "And where's the eye patch and parrot?" She looked him over. "Then again, maybe you *should* let Neeley see you in that. She's odd enough, she might like it."

Roland didn't let her puncture his enthusiasm. "It's got to be some place warm or else they have given me something more to wear right? On the water. Warm weather. Weapons!"

"Axe and sword," Ivar noted.

Roland smiled. "Yeah!"

"That's a boarding axe," Eagle said. "It served an array of functions on a sailing ship. Damage control in case of fire. Also to cut through enemy boarding nets and lines. And to cut away fouled rigging. Technically not as effective a weapon as a musket or pistol but—" he'd already lost Roland's attention because the big man had noted something more interesting.

"Is that a forty-five under your coat?" Roland asked Ivar.

"Oh no," Scout muttered, but they were all saved as Moms entered.

"Pretty spiffy," Scout said.

Moms was dressed in a grey business suit, end of World War II era and the years after. The waist was cinched in tight, her heels were raised but not technically high and her short hair was done up in some way that was actually quite striking.

"You look good," Roland said, in only the way Roland could say such a thing. Honest and blunt without subtext.

"Thank you, Roland," Moms said. She noted Scout. "No hot water, eh?"

There wasn't any time to discuss weapons or clothing or hot water further as the door to the interior of the Possibility Palace opened and Dane came in, followed by Lara and Edith Frobish.

"Let's get to it," Dane said, picking up a piece of chalk, going to the blackboard.

"We don't get a kiss first?" Scout said. "Small talk?"

Dane wrote in bold letters at the top:

14 FEBRUARY

He turned to her. "No. But you get the man the day is named after. Saint Valentine."

He wrote:

278 AD

"What did he do?" Scout asked. "Give out a lot of chocolate? Roses?"

"He got his head cut off," Dane said.

"Oh," Scout said. "That's not good."

"That's why he's known as a martyr," Edith explained, "and was anointed a saint in the Catholic Church."

Dane nodded at Edith to continue with the briefing.

"Not much is known about Saint Valentine of Terni, as he is officially recorded. In fact, the name might represent three different real men: a priest from Rome, or perhaps the Bishop of Terni. Or, even, although doubtful, a man who was killed in northern Africa along with several other Catholic missionaries."

"Vague much," Scout said.

Edith was used to Scout's ways. "The bubble is in Italy. Along the Via Flaminia, also known as the Ravenna Road. Near the Milvian Bridge, which is where Saint Valentine was reported to have been killed. There are various stories as to why he was killed, the most popular being that he continued to secretly marry Christians in defiance of the Roman Emperor's decree forbidding it. But no one truly knows and the reality is, like many myths, some of what actually happened was co-opted later by others and rewritten."

Eagle spoke up. "Chaucer said Valentines Day was when 'every fowl comes forth to cho0se his mate'."

"How romantic," Scout said, causing Edith and Eagle to exchange an embarrassed look. Scout turned serious. "So? What am I supposed to do? Make sure he dies?"

"No idea," Dane said.

"We've done vague before," Scout said, "but this is really vague. You're not even sure it's one guy. Could be two? Could be three?"

"The Shadow is opening a bubble in a specific place and time," Dane said. "It's something. Also--" he hesitated, which was unusual.

Moms and Eagle exchanged glances.

"What's going on?" Moms asked.

"Nothing," Dane said.

"Right," Scout said, but didn't ask any more questions and Dane didn't give anyone else a chance to chime in as he wrote:

1945

He pointed the chalk at Eagle, then at Doc. "You're both going to the same year. Different places, of course. We've had that before, when Roland and Ivar both went to 1863. Doc, you're going to be a POW. In Germany."

Eagle's prodigious memory had already solved that. "Dresden."

Dane nodded. "Indeed."

"I do not like the sound of that," Doc said, glancing between Eagle and Dane.

"The Dresden firebombing," Edith said. "A horrible event, one that some say was a war crime. However, the reality is that in the scope of all the bombing missions in World War II, it wasn't even close to being the deadliest although the justification for targeting Dresden was called into question."

"Let's not forget a couple of nukes dropped later that year," Doc said.

"We're not here to debate the morality of—" Dane began, but everyone was surprised when Lara cut in.

"Why not?"

"Because it happened," Dane said. "It's history."

"Which the Shadow is trying to change," Lara said.

"We don't know what exactly the Shadow is trying to change," Dane said. "It's doubtful there's anything it could do to stop the firebombing. Even if it did, what difference would that make in the long run?"

"A lot of people live?" Lara suggested.

"That day," Dane said. "But what about the day after? And the day after?" He shook his head. "I think it's going after something else."

"Vonnegut?" Eagle said.

Edith nodded. "Possible."

"What?" Doc was with most of the team members: confused.

"Kurt Vonnegut," Edith said. "A writer. He wrote *Slaughterhouse Five* largely based on his experience in Dresden as a POW. And since we know from the intel we have that you need to go as a POW there's a good chance you'll be the same place as him."

Eagle chimed in. "He survived the firebombing because he and his fellow POWs were being held in a slaughterhouse and they took refuge in an underground meat locker."

"This is not sounding very good at all," Doc said.

"When does it ever?" Scout said.

"Why would this Vonnegut guy be important?" Moms asked, deflecting attention from Scout.

Edith replied. "He's considered one of literature's more important 20th century American writers, but overall—" she shrugged.

"As always," Dane said, "we don't quite know why you're going there other than to preserve history."

"The Dresden Firebombing was quite controversial," Edith said. "There are many who believe it wasn't justified. It was the first time the public in the Allied countries questioned some of what they were doing to win the war. Many thought the bombing wasn't essential to the war effort."

"You have to remember," Moms argued, "that the Allies were still reeling from the Battle of the Bulge. To that point, they'd considered the war almost over. The German offensive surprised everyone."

Eagle added: "In fact, Vonnegut was captured during the Battle of the Bulge."

Dane held up a hand. "Second-guessing military actions is easy from the cheap seats. We're talking Nazi Germany. So let's leave that aside and—"

"Why?" Lara asked. "So we can just follow orders? That sounds a bit, what's the word? Nazi?"

Dane slapped his hand on the table. "This is an operational briefing. Not a debate. If the Shadow succeeds, there won't be any more debating. Ever. Keep that in mind. Always. I *know* that for a fact."

Lara appeared ready to say something, but Moms shook her head and the young girl slumped back in her chair.

Dane waited, one second, two, then turned back to the blackboard. He underlined:

1945

"Eagle. You're going to the *USS Quincy* on the Great Bitter Lake for—"

Eagle finished for him. "The meeting between President Roosevelt and King Abdul Ibn Saud."

Dane nodded. "Exactly."

Eagle indicated his attire. "Mess steward?"

"Yes," Dane said. "But you were picked because—"

This time Moms interrupted Dane. "Eagle can speak Arabic."

"Exactly," Dane said. "On the surface it might have made more sense to have you go to Dresden, but the natural language ability over-rides that. Even though we can put languages in your download, there's also your innate understanding of the context of history. This meeting is largely overlooked, occurring as Roosevelt was on the way back from the much more famous Yalta Conference with Stalin and Churchill, but it was extremely significant in shaping events in the Middle East, and thus the world, to the present day."

"It was the beginning of the rise of the Middle East oil states," Eagle said. "Prior to World War II, the United States had been one of the leading oil producers in the world; in fact, a large reason the Japanese attacked the US at Pearl Harbor was because we'd sanctioned them on oil."

"There is also," Edith said, "the issue of a homeland for the Jewish people after the War. Roosevelt and Saud covered many topics."

"A lot happened in those brief meetings on that ship between Roosevelt and King Saud," Dane said. "Given that Roosevelt would be dead in less than two months, it was one of the last important meetings he had, but it set the groundwork for a lot of future history."

"Whoa," Scout said. "Run that by me again?"

"Future history," Dane said. "Future from the date of the mission; history from the perspective of the present."

"Okay," Scout said. "Sort of makes senses."

"Do we have any idea what the Shadow is trying to change?" Eagle asked.

"No," Dane said. "But we believe an Agent-In-Time is on the ship. So you'll get some help."

"How do I know who the agent is?" Eagle asked.

"He'll know who you are," Dane said.

"How do you know it's a he?" Lara asked.

"It's a U.S. warship in World War II," Dane said. "There were no women on the *Quincy* or with Roosevelt's entourage."

"If *he* isn't an agent of the Shadow," Scout pointed out. "Never know who you're going to run into. Might try to kill you. Or a guy saving you from the first guy trying to kill you, might also try to kill you. It's complicated."

"He might," Dane said, surprising everyone. "Who knows? I don't. Do you think I like sending you on these missions with obviously inadequate intelligence? But it's all we have." He took a step away from the board toward the team. "I went on ops in Vietnam with even less intelligence than you're getting here. Where 'vague much' was an understatement," he added, looking at Scout.

Moms spoke up. "We know you're doing all you can." She paused. "But are you telling us everything?"

"I'm telling you what I can," Dane said. "What you need to know for your missions. I give you my word on that."

"So what aint you telling us?" Lara asked. "What don't we need to know? More importantly, how do *you* know *we* don't need to know it?"

Dane turned on her. "Why don't you tell us about you? Where did you come from? How did you get on that Russian plane?"

Lara didn't blink. "I wish I could. I don't know exactly. I have no idea. Good enough?"

"No," Dane said, "I think you're lying."

"If I am," Lara said, with a slight smile, "it's because you don't have a need to know."

"All right," Moms interjected. "Let's calm down."

"You're not even going on a mission," Dane said to Lara.

"Then why I am here?" Lara asked.

Everyone was surprised when Edith spoke. "Because you have a need to know."

Lara was surprised. "What?"

Edith continued in her low, calm voice. "You don't know who you are or where you came from. We don't know either. But you're here. We think that's for a reason. We have no idea what that reason is, but we're trusting it's a good one."

Lara glanced at Scout, who shrugged.

"All right," Lara said. "That makes as much sense as anything."

"Something else," Dane said. "Since we have had a loop between missions before, I've directed Edith to add a basic briefing on each other's missions in your download. Just in case that might turn out to be another loop where one mission could affect the other."

"That makes sense," Eagle said.

Dane shifted to Moms. "You're going to the year after Doc and Eagle." He wrote on the board.

1946

"Edith," Dane said, giving her the floor.

"E.N.I.A.C.," Edith said, pronouncing each letter was such reverence one knew each was capitalized.

Moms raised an eyebrow, waiting.

"A computer," Ivar supplied.

"One of the first," Doc added. "A Turing-complete, digital computer. In essence a huge calculator capable of computing complex math problems faster than humans could. It was a big step forward in the early days of computing."

"Okay," Moms said. "And I'm going there why?"

Edith continued. "While Turing's computer during World War II was kept under wraps because of Enigma, ENIAC was formally introduced to the public on the Fifteenth of February, 1946. The press called it the 'Great Brain'. The project was initiated by the military in 1943 to design a machine capable of rapidly calculating artillery trajectories under a secret project code-named Project PX."

"ENIAC could branch," Doc said, pronouncing it as one word. "Trigger different operations depending on the result of the previous operation. That was a new development."

"Right," Moms said again. She looked at Dane. "I have no idea what that means. Why am I going on this mission and not one of them?" She indicated Doc and Ivar.

Edith answered. "Because of the ENIAC Six. They've been mostly forgotten by history, but the six people who designed the programming for the computer were women."

"Like those women who programmed the early computers at NASA?" Moms said.

"Well before them," Edith said. "The ENIAC Six were computing pioneers. The ENIAC, while it took up an entire room, didn't have any memory. It was essentially a bunch of adding machines connected by cables. It had to be programmed by hand to set various tables of numbers. This came down to setting twelve hundred ten-way switches. Something, apparently, no man had the patience to figure out. So they gave the work to six women. In fact, prior to this, because of the shortage of manpower due to the war, and the requirements of the war—" Edith was rushing her words in her excitement at telling this story of history—"the Army had recruited women for positions, and they really called the people this: 'computers'. Who could calculate artillery trajectories by hand. These six women were given the blueprints of ENIAC and the wiring diagrams and told to figure out how to make the machine work."

"Wait a second," Moms said. "You're saying they built a machine but didn't know how to make it work?"

"The engineers who built it," Edith said, "knew *how* it worked in theory. They just didn't know how to physically program it for use. That required the women to analyze equations, then patch together the correct cables and then set all those ten-way switches. And deal with all the bugs and shorts. The ENIAC used around eighteen thousand vacuum tubes so they were constantly burning out. It was incredible what they managed to achieve, yet when it was announced, people assumed the women in the press photos were models; not the people who'd figured it out."

"So I'm going the day before that press conference," Moms said. "Like Scout went to UCLA in '69 for the first Internet message. To make sure the thing works?"

"We assume that," Dane said, "but you know how I feel about assumptions."

Doc held up a hand. "Is this tied to our research trying to make a Turing Time Calculator? That's how Ivar and I know about ENIAC. We went back to the basics stemming from Turing's early work. Does the Shadow know we're trying to figure out where they're going to attack next? What the pattern is?"

"How are you doing on that?" Lara asked. "Trying to predict the future?"

Doc frowned. "We haven't been able to discern a pattern to the attacks yet."

"Given there have only been five days," Ivar said, "with six attacks each, that's not much data."

"Do you want more data?" Lara asked, her tone indicating what she thought of that.

"All right," Dane said. "Let's keep on target here. Right now, it's good enough that we can track the disturbances in the timeline in the Pit and via our agents in the various times. We know where the Shadow is opening bubbles for Valentines Day. Let's keep our focus on the immediate problem which is the mission."

He ended the discussion by writing the next year on the board.

1779

"Roland," Dane said. "This is yours. Kealakekua Bay, the Big Island of Hawaii."

"Cool," Roland said. "I've only passed through Hawaii on deployments."

"It's not a vacation," Dane said.

Roland held up the boarding axe. "I figured that. And this will be another passing through."

"On the fourteenth of February, 1779, Captain James Cook of the Royal Navy, was killed by natives," Dane said.

Edith threw in her facts. "Cook is known for being the first European to reach the east coast of Australia and the first to find Hawaii. He also extensively explored the Pacific Northwest coast of North America, searching for a Northwest Passage."

"But he did all that *before* he died," Roland pointed out. "Why am I going to the day he dies? The Shadow going to try to save him? Why?"

"We don't know," Dane said.

"Cook wasn't the only one killed," Edith said. "Some native Hawaiians died. And some survived from his crew who later made history. Captain Bligh, who would later command the *HMS Bounty*, was Cook's sailing master. He was there."

"So I just keep my eyes and ears open and see what's not quite right," Roland summed up his mission. "It could have nothing to do with Cook. Like what happened in Germany on my last trip had nothing to do with Varus or Arminius." He pointed the boarding axe toward the monster's scale on the wall. "Could be Grendels and such."

"Correct," Dane said.

"All right," Roland said.

Dane wrote the last mission on the board.

1929

"Ivar."

"Not the mob again," Ivar protested, but there was no energy in it. The clothes, the gun, the date, all added up.

"Chicago this time," Dane said.

Even Ivar knew what that location and the date meant. "The Saint Valentines Day massacre."

Dane gave Edith the go-ahead. "You'll get all the specifics in the download, but the fundamentals of the massacre are that seven men were killed inside a garage on the North Side of Chicago. Five were members of George 'Bugs' Moran's gang. Two others, a gang associate and a mechanic, were also among the dead.

"It is highly likely, although never conclusively proved, that the killers were sent by Al Capone. There were four men, two dressed as police and two with Thompson submachine guns who entered the garage. They lined the seven up against a wall, then gunned them down. One victim survived for a few hours. When asked who did it, he told the police 'no one shot me'."

Ivar spread his hands. "I don't get it. What am I supposed to do? Make sure they get killed? The same with Roland and Captain Cook. And Scout and Saint Valentine. These missions are messed up."

"We didn't invent them," Dane said. "Remember, the Shadow uses misdirection. The event each day is known for might not be the Shadow's target."

"What if I go into my bubble," Ivar said, "and I'm one of the guys lined up against the wall? I got cement overshoes last time I went to 1929."

"You'll figure it out," Dane said.

"Vague much," Scout said.

"Scout," Eagle warned, stepping in as team sergeant.

"Listen," Dane said. "I agree with you. We have to accept that as we adapt, the Shadow adapts. And the other timelines. Ivar's mission to Chile on Nine Eleven was different. He rescued Dominic, who was from another timeline. But as a result of that mission, a loop was closed, with Dominic disappearing from here. So the question we have to wonder about is whether that bubble in Chile was an attempt to change our timeline or to fix a problem the Shadow had from *another* timeline?"

"I think," Ivar said, "that the problem in that incident wasn't with the Shadow, but with Pandora's timeline of Gaia. Dominic and his mother were refugees from that timeline."

Dane nodded. "Possibly. We know there are other players, other timelines, in this war with the Shadow. With their own agendas. Pandora and her ilk from the Gaia timeline. The Fates. The minions of the Shadow like the Legion and the Spartan mercenaries from their timeline."

"Monsters," Roland threw in.

"Yes," Dane said. "Grendels and Aglaeca. Yeti. Kraken. And the Valkyries. There's an infinite number of possible timelines. Many are unaffected by Gates, going along without interference. Our best guess is that the Shadow is the one that managed to open Gates first and was able to travel between timelines. And they developed time travel. Because of that, they gained tremendous power. They've destroyed a number of timelines, raped them for their natural resources, destroyed others that were a threat, like mine. Subjugated others, such as the one nominally ruled by the Spartans."

"What's the Shadow's end game?" Lara asked.

"If we knew that," Dane said, "we might be able to anticipate what it's going to do. Then again, maybe it doesn't have an end game beyond survival."

"Like us," Lara said.

Dane walked forward, between where Moms and Eagle were seated and leaned forward. He put his fists on the top of the table as he spoke. "We're swinging in the dark. Fighting back against the bubbles the Shadow is punching in our past. We know the Shadow is trying to cause changes in history. Ripples. A big enough Ripple will be a Cascade. And six Cascades; well that initiates the Rule of Seven. The seventh event being a Time Tsunami that wipes this timeline out.

We know that's happened to other timelines." Dane straightened, taking his hands off the table. "That's what we're dealing with. If that's not enough—" he didn't say anything further.

Moms stood. "It's good enough, Dane. Scout and Lara are upset. I told Frasier not to enter the team bunk area after catching him there, watching Lara while she slept. He did it again. That's not acceptable. He told them he was doing it on your orders."

Dane nodded. "He's trying to find out the truth about Lara's background based on my orders. But I agree. Entering your team sanctum, especially after being warned not to, is unacceptable. You have my word it will not happen again. I've already dealt with him regarding that."

"Are you done?" Moms asked Dane and Edith.

"Not quite." Dane looked at Edith.

"In regard to Doc's question," Edith said. "There's more to the Saint Valentines Day Massacre. No one was ever convicted of perpetrating the crime. But it is widely accepted the shooters were sent by Al Capone. Two of the suspected shooters, you'll get the names in your download, were killed not long afterward. Perhaps Capone covering his tracks. As far as is known, nobody involved in this, including Capone, had a happy ending."

"I'm only there for twenty-four hours," Ivar pointed out.

"There's something else strange about it," Edith said. "One of the men killed was Jimmy Clark, Bugs Moran's brother-in-law and second-in-command. His real name was Kachellek, but he went by the alias of Clark. For the rest of his life, Capone swore that Clark's ghost haunted him. He would scream Clark's name in the middle of the night, to the point where bodyguards would break in, worried their boss was being attacked. In prison, he was known to cry out for Clark to leave him alone. Now that could be ascribed to Capone's mind deteriorating from his syphilis, which eventually reduced his mental capacity to that of a child, but as we know, there are other explanations for ghosts and visions."

"Why would the Shadow send a Valkyrie to haunt Capone?" Ivar asked.

"I don't know," Edith said. "But it just struck me as odd." She was flustered, but Moms came to her aid.

"A lot of this is guesswork and acting on gut instinct," Moms said. "We have to pay attention to that instinct."

Edith nodded. "It's also odd that Kurt Vonnegut is located where and when Doc is going. His novel, largely based on that experience, *Slaughterhouse Five*, has time travel in it."

"A ripple?" Eagle asked.

"Or just his imagination," Dane said.

"What about the other missions?" Moms asked Edith, ignoring Dane. "Anything strike you as odd? Or, I should say, odder than usual?"

Edith glanced at Dane and he gave a slight nod. She pulled a flat plastic bag out of her leather satchel. "This will help you, Ivar." She put it on the table in front of him.

Ivar looked at it but didn't touch it. "What is it?"

"A letter of introduction."

"What?" Ivar said. "From who to who?"

"From Meyer Lansky to Alfonso Capone," Edith said.

Ivar stared at her. "No."

Edith swallowed, but didn't say anything.

"You're joking right?" Ivar said. "A letter of introduction? Who is it introducing?"

Dane intervened. "You."

The rest of the team stared at Ivar. He closed his eyes. "I met Lansky on 29 October 1929. I'm going back to 14 February 1929. Before then. How can Lansky know who I am before he meets me?"

Edith struggled to answer. "He wrote the letter *after* he met you."

"But as far as he knows, he killed me," Ivar said. "I don't understand this at all. Why would he write a letter of recommendation for someone he put concrete shoes on?"

Edith turned to Dane.

Ivar continued. "Why would he even write such a letter anyway?"

Dane indicated the letter. "We've got it. Edith went through a lot of trouble to track it down so quickly and get it here."

"Bull," Lara said. Everyone turned toward her. "You're telling me you learned of this bubble just several hours ago and then managed to find this letter? You had it. You had it all along."

The deep red blanketing Edith's face betrayed the truth about the lie. Moms glanced at Eagle, then faced Dane. "Truth. Now."

"We had it," Dane admitted. "Except we didn't know we had it."

"Clarify," Moms snapped.

Dane spread his hands, indicating the Possibility Palace. "There's more to this place than the Time Pit. We've got archives. Yes, the filing cabinets along the Spiral are full of scrolls of information. All of recorded history. Key information. But we've got caverns surrounding this place full of artifacts and more documents gathered over the years by our agents. It's catalogued, but by hand and on paper, because—"

"No computers," Doc said. "You've never explained that."

"Anything electronic can be hacked," Dane said. "It's that simple." He indicated Eagle. "You received a transmission to shut down your electronics during your last mission, didn't you?"

"You know I did," Eagle said. "You were in the debrief."

Dane nodded. "Same thing I got in my timeline when I was in Vietnam on the mission to recover the black box."

"What black box?" Eagle asked.

Dane dismissed that with a wave. "It's not important. My timeline. Which is gone. The message is the key. It came from the Ones Before. We don't know who they are, but they help. Once in a while. The Shadow can track electronic signals. Much better than we can. We do know of one timeline where the Shadow attacked via the Internet. A timeline where computers had developed earlier and the Internet much faster. Where control for everything had been given over to their form of the Internet. Once the Shadow took control, it was easy to wipe that timeline out. We're not taking any chances here."

"*Battlestar Gallactica*," Eagle murmured.

"Frak that," Scout acknowledged.

"Back to the note," Moms said.

"We have archives," Dane continued. "Once the alert was sounded for this mission, our analysts begin going through the archive records. They found the note. It's that simple."

"Then why lie about it?" Ivar asked.

"Because we're wasting time here," Dane said. "The Gates for your bubbles open soon. I can't detail everything. You'll get the pertinent data in your download."

"I still don't understand how Lansky can write a note to Capone," Ivar had the letter out and was reading it, "telling him I'm trustworthy, when he thinks I'm dead."

"Because," Dane said, "he knew you weren't killed."

"And how did he know that?" Ivar asked.

"Because of you," Dane said. "It's your fault. You violated the rules of Time Patrol. You told Lansky who you were."

"I had to," Ivar argued. "You guys gave me money printed *after* the time I was sent to on Black Tuesday."

"Yes, yes," Dane said. "I know. Our fault. It's why we let your violation go. But we had to contain the Ripple that caused. Lansky knew part of his future. You told him he would die a natural death. So we had an agent contact him. He found out you weren't dead. We got some things from him. The note was one of them."

Ivar shook his head. "Still doesn't make sense. How did you know you would need this note?"

"We didn't," Dane said. He sighed. "But apparently our Agent-In-Time did. Our best guess is the A-I-T knows about *this* mission you're going on and went to Lansky *afterward* and got him to write it."

"That's a loop," Doc pointed out.

"Indeed," Dane said. "Much like your mission to Philly in 1776 on Independence Day was a loop to Moms' mission to Monticello in 1826. One affected the other. It happens."

"My head hurts," Roland said.

"I understand," Dane said. "It's not easy. But it is what it is. We need to get going."

"You mean *we* need to get going," Moms clarified.

"Of course," Dane said.

"Can we have a team moment?" Moms asked.

"Certainly." Dane led Edith out of the team room, shutting the door behind him.

Moms turned to the team. "More than ever, we have to hold on to some of our traditions as a team. Those of us who were Nightstalkers were inculcated into some traditions. I don't know when they began. Before I got there. Before even Nada," she said, nodding toward the name etched on the table. "But they give us stability. They give us continuity."

She looked around the table, meeting each person's gaze for a moment before moving on to the next.

"We're getting distracted," she said. "I know this is confusing. But that's the nature of war. Organized chaos. This is more chaotic than what we're used to. I don't pretend to understand the loops and how each affects the other. Let's get back to basics.

"Why are we here?" Moms looked around the table at the Team. "Because, as Dane said, we are the last defense against the Shadow. We man the walls surrounding our timeline. We live and fight in a realm which ordinary people have no clue exists. This place—" she pointed down— "the Possibility Palace, is something many couldn't even imagine. Most people are worried about ordinary things. Paying the mortgage. Taking care of their family. Their job. We have a higher calling.

"We stand watch. We protect them. Both their worries and their joys. We keep the Shadow from wiping them, everyone, out of existence. None of us know exactly what we're going to face when we go through the Gate into the time bubble the Shadow has created. We've run five missions. We've stopped the Shadow on every one. We'll do it again." She turned to Eagle, who stood up next to her.

"It is protocol for us to acknowledge our fallen team-mates because no one else will," Eagle said. "Their names were erased when they joined the team, whether it be the Nightstalkers or the Time Patrol. We must pay respect and give honors." Eagle reached out and touched the top of the table, running his hand over the first name. "He was named Nada by the team, the Nighstalkers, when he joined them. In death he regains his name and his past. He was Master Sergeant Edward Moreno, Delta Force. He left behind a wife and a daughter. We look after his daughter, Isabella, because we always look after our own, just as we will look after any family member. He made the choice to go back and right a wrong."

Lara looked surprised by that, glancing over at Scout, but Eagle was already moving on. "He was named Mac by the team, but he was Sergeant First Class Eric Bowen, U.S. Army Special Forces, MOS eighteen-charlie, engineer—"

"Best damn demo man ever," Roland muttered.

"—from the great state of Texas. He made the ultimate sacrifice for his country, for his world, for his timeline during the D-Day mission. We speak his rank and name as it was."

The team said as one: "Sergeant First Class Eric Bowen."

Scout looked over at Lara. "As long as a name is remembered, we live on."

The team sergeant spoke the words they'd all heard before. "We are here because the best of intentions can go horribly awry and the worst of intentions can achieve exactly what it sets out to do. It is often the noblest scientific inquiry that can produce the end of us all. We are here because we are the last defense when the desire to do right turns into a wrong. We are here because mankind advances through trial and error. Because nothing man does is ever perfect. And we are ultimately here because the Shadow is out there, trying to obliterate us. That is our duty."

Moms finished. "Can we all live with that?"

The Team moved out, heading for their Gates.

Left alone, Lara waited until the door shut, then she spoke quite clearly. "No. I can't live with that.

The Missions Phase I

"I am like any other man. All I do is supply a demand."

—Al Capone

Chicago, 14 February 1929 A.D.

IVAR WASN'T THERE, and then he was there, but he'd sort of always been there. It was the best way to explain how he arrived, becoming part of his current time and place without fanfare or excitement among those around him; well, not exactly, because the guy sitting across the table from him twitched his hand, lifting up a folded newspaper, revealing a .45 caliber pistol pointed at Ivar.

Ivar was in the bubble of this day, not before, and hopefully not afterward, as long as this guy didn't shoot him.

It is 1929 A.D. The Museum of Modern Art opens in New York City; All Quiet on the Western Front *is published;* Popeye *appears for the first time in a comic; the first patent for color television is submitted; Mother Teresa arrives in Calcutta to begin her work among India's poorest; Grand Teton National Park is established by President Calvin Coolidge; Herbert Hoover then becomes president and the first telephone is installed at the White House; the yo-yo is introduced; the British High Court rules that Canadian women are persons; the New York Yankees become the first team to put numbers on their uniforms; the longest bridge in the world, the San Francisco Bay Toll, opens; President Hoover proposes the Kellogg-Briand Pact, which renounces war; the first US roller coaster is built; Lieutenant James Doolittle flies over Mitchell Field in New York in the first all instrument flight; the Peking Man skull is found; Palestinians and Jews riot over control of the Western Wall and over one hundred are killed.*

Doc had been to this year before. And met mobsters before, specifically Bugsy Seigal and Meyer Lansky in New York City. And ended up wearing cement shoes and being dumped in Long Island Sound. This looked like it might end before it even got started.

Some things change; some don't.

"You got the note?" the man asked.

Ivar took a moment to get oriented. He was in a café. Mostly empty. An old man sitting on a stool at the counter. A cook in the kitchen. An old waitress leaning on a wall in the far corner, staring wistfully out of the window at the quiet street where a light snow was falling. And the guy with the gun.

"Yes."

"Cough it up."

Ivar reached for the inside coat pocket.

"Easy!" the man said, catching a glimpse of the holstered gun.

Ivar carefully slid the note out and put it on the table.

With his free hand, the man took it. He unfolded it with some difficulty, still keeping the gun at the ready.

He read it. Slowly, lips moving. "That's got to be it." He holstered the gun in a shoulder holster and smiled. "Guess this means I'm gonna be alive for a while yet."

"Who are you?" Ivar asked.

The man shook the note. "I'm the guy whose gonna get Meyer Lansky to write this some time after today, right?"

"Is that a question?"

"Is that an answer?"

"I don't understand," Ivar said.

"Makes two of us." The guy grinned. "I don't either, buddy." There was a light in his eyes, and it took Ivar a moment, then it clicked. Crazy eyes.

The man began reading the note again, his forehead furrowed in concentration. "I gotta remember this."

Crazy eyes and dumb. Not a good combination in Ivar's experience.

Done, the man folded the note and gave it back. "So you're Ivar?"

"It's in the note."

"Yeah. Got that. Capone's out of town. At his joint in Florida. Bugs and his guys are supposed to meet in the garage down the street. Then some of them are heading to Detroit to get a shipment of booze."

"It's a set up," Ivar said.

The man grinned again, his eyes dancing. "You know that? Yeah, guess you would. Bugs is so stupid he thinks the Purple Gang in Detroit is gonna sell him some booze on the cheap? Even though Moran knows Al owns them? Dumb as a rock. Deserves to die."

"Yeah," Ivar said. "And you are?"

"Strings."

"Excuse me?"

"They call me Strings."

Ivar was checking the download but there was no mention of a 'Strings'. Edith had missed something. Or, Ivar realized, left something out. If Strings was a Time Patrol A-I-T, then maybe Ivar didn't have a need to know.

Not fraking likely, Ivar thought.

Strings reached into a pocket and pulled out a piece of piano wire, two feet long, with a piece of wood on each end. "One of my strings," he said. "I'm up to eighteen now. So that's the, what you call it, plurals, of string. Strings. I like doing my jobs close and personal like."

"Okay," Ivar said, for lack of anything else. Something occurred to him. "If Capone is out of town, why did I need the note?"

"I needed it," Strings said. "To make sure you is who you say you is."

Maybe not so dumb, Ivar thought.

Strings indicated the shoulder holster. "You good with that piece you're packing?"

"I can shoot," Ivar said. He had spent time on the range at Bragg. He also remembered the barely restrained looks of disgust among the instructors about his lack of martial talent. He'd sent bullets down range. Some had even hit targets.

"How about a Chicago typewriter?"

"A what?" Download supplied definition. "A Thompson submachine gun?"

"Yeah. A tommy-gun. Rat-a-tat-tat-tat."

"I've fired one," Ivar said, "but I'm not proficient." As soon as he said it, Ivar regretted it, because he realized what he'd just done.

"Okay, fair enough," Strings said. "Not like Tony or Sam is gonna give up their blaster anyways."

"Where are the others?" Ivar asked.

"Around." Strings nodded toward a phone hanging on the wall. "We'll call them when the time is right."

Which was supposed to be when Bugs Moran arrived, except he didn't. That was the way history was supposed to play out. The question was: how was the Shadow trying to change this? And why? Who cared about these psychopathic gangsters? What if Moran did show up and was killed today? Would that change anything important?

Ivar knew what Dane would make of his mental gymnastics and decided not to waste any more time on it. He slumped back in the booth, now somewhat aware of his role for the day. The odor wafting out of the kitchen caused his stomach to rumble. "Can I get breakfast first?"

"Sure. Then we deliver a bloody Valentine."

"Men are not prisoners of fate, but prisoners of their own mind."
—President Franklin Roosevelt

The Great Bitter Lake, 14 February 1945 A.D.

EAGLE WASN'T THERE, and then he was there, but he'd always sort of been there. It was the best way to explain how he arrived, becoming part of his current time and place without fanfare or excitement, which was irrelevant, since there was no one else around him. He was in the bubble of this day, not before, and hopefully he wouldn't be here afterward.

Truly, because the immediate 'there' was a tight enclosed space and Eagle wasn't a fan of that unless he had the controls for an aircraft in front of him.

He was in a gray, steel room, barely big enough for his large frame, and as he turned, he hit his head on a crossbeam. Stifling a curse, Eagle put his hands on the wheel to open the hatch. It was stifling hot in the room, easily over one hundred degrees.

The wheel didn't budge.

The only light came from a dim, grimy bulb, which was flickering uncertainly.

Eagle closed his eyes and tried to control his breathing in a conscious attempt to regulate his heart rate, which was beating more rapidly than he would have preferred.

It is 1945 A.D.. Rod Stewart is born; War correspondent Joseph Morton becomes the only Allied reporter executed by the Axis; Audie Murphy wins the Medal of Honor; Auschwitz and Birkenau are liberated; the Burma Road opens; the Zionist World Congress asks the British government to found Israel, Britain demurs for the time being; the Yalta Conference between Roosevelt, Stalin and Churchill tries to establish a post-war Europe; Arthur C. Clarke introduces the concept of a geosynchronous communications satellite.

Eagle was trapped inside metal, unable to escape

Some things change; some don't.

Eagle opened his eyes, his heart rate, almost, but not quite, normal. He could feel the slight sway in the deck, indicating he was likely on the *Quincy*. It was going to be a long twenty-four hours if he couldn't get out of this place.

The wheel suddenly turned and Eagle tensed.

The hatch opened and a man in uniform was silhouetted in the brighter passageway light.

"Strange," the man said, looking Eagle up and down. "Not what I expected, but I wasn't sure what to expect, so I suppose that makes sense."

Eagle's eyes adjusted. The man was an Army general. There was a Silver Star at the top of the ribbons on his chest, some of which Eagle didn't immediately recognize but assumed were service ribbons from World War II and dating back to World War I, given the man's age.

The download was spitting up information about service ribbons but Eagle skipped those and locked identity into place: General Edwin 'Pa' Watson. President Roosevelt's Military Advisor and Appointments Secretary. In essence, his Chief of Staff.

"General," Eagle said, uncertain how to proceed since this was the first time he'd been met by a Time Patrol agent on one of his missions. He also remembered that on Scout's first mission the 'agent' had turned out to be an assassin working for the Shadow.

Watson took a step back, allowing Eagle to exit the small enclosure.

The passageway was empty, but voices echoed from the deck above. The throb of engines reverberated through the ship.

"King Saud will be on-board shortly," Watson said. "Why are you here? What's going to happen?"

The way he phrased the latter question and the fact he'd known Eagle was in the compartment, indicated the meeting was more than chance, but Eagle wasn't certain. "You were expecting me, sir?"

"I was expecting someone," Watson said.

"Why?" Eagle asked.

"I was told someone would be here a very long time ago."

"How long ago?"

Watson's eyes went vacant for a moment, accessing memory in a foggy brain. "After I resigned from the Academy in oh-four."

The download confirmed that Watson had taken six years to make it through the four year program at West Point: he'd been discharged in his plebe year for failing math; then re-admitted. Then he'd resigned in 1904, but came back the following summer. After entering with the class of 1906, he'd finally graduated with the class of 1908, a year before George S. Patton.

"Who did you meet?" Eagle asked.

"An old woman," Watson said.

"And she told you I would be here? On this ship? Today?"

Watson nodded. "Yes. Forty-one years ago. Today. Fourteen February. Nineteen-oh-four. I was on the Plain. Done with it all. Already resigned from the Academy. Standing at Trophy Point, bidding my Rockbound Highland home adieu. And she was there. In a robe. With a staff. And she told me the path I was choosing, thought I was choosing, was not my path. It was not my choice." He grimaced. "Imagine that? I thought she was some crackpot, but then she told me things, things no one else could have known." He locked down briefly. "Secrets." He looked back up. "She told me what I must do—go back into the Academy and graduate. And she told me of things to come." Watson grimaced. "Every single one has come true.

"And now I'm meeting you. In retrospect, I believe that was the correct choice, given all that has transpired since. I'm here today, on board this ship with the President, and now you're here."

Watson didn't look well. His skin was pale, his shoulders slumped. The download indicated he would be dead in six days. Cerebral hemorrhage while the ship was off the coast of Algiers on its way back to the States; presaging Roosevelt's death by a few months.

"Do you know who the old woman was?" Watson asked.

Eagle had a very good idea—a Fate, which added a troubling variable to this mission. "No."

"Why are you here?" Watson didn't seem very enthusiastic. "What are you? A cook?"

"I'm a pilot," Eagle said. "And a soldier."

Watson nodded. "I imagine things are different where you're from. I guess I should say *when* you're from. But, Negroes are serving now with distinction on all fronts. It is to be expected that will continue and expand. I don't suppose you want to tell me when you are from?"

"I can't."

"Yes," Watson said. "The rules. Always rules. But rules are important. You know the President has a rule. He can't be photographed in the chair. So I have to hold him up. Either me or his son, but James is in the Marines now." Once more his gaze grew vacant. "The President bears such a heavy burden. I wonder who will help him if I can't."

"Why do you say that?" Eagle asked.

Watson reached out and put a shaking hand on Eagle's shoulder. "I'm ill, son. You can see that. So is Franklin. I don't think either of us has much longer. I just hope I can last long enough to keep the President standing. Because the country is going to need him to stand. Especially once he uses that A-bomb if those fellows in Los Alamos ever get the damn thing working. Oppenheimer says there will be nothing left of Berlin but ash. But I suppose you know the answer to how that turns out."

Eagle did. They'd get it working.

But Berlin wasn't supposed to be the target.

"It is natural for people to behave in a loving way."
—Hawaiian saying

Hawaii, 14 February 1779 A.D.

ROLAND WASN'T THERE, and then he was there, but he'd sort of always been there. It was the best way to explain how he arrived, becoming part of his current time and place without fanfare or excitement among those around him, although Roland was ready for an attack from any direction.

Which was the way Roland always arrived and a good thing, because a figure came running up out of the dark along a jungle path toward him. The man was dressed in a naval uniform, of higher standing than Roland since he had a buttoned shirt and frock coat and shoes.

"Help!" the officer called out.

Chasing the officer were two native Hawaiian men, clubs raised.

Roland pulled the cutlass and raised the boarding axe. Each weapon took a blow from a club as the Hawaiians focused their rage on him. The blows staggered Roland back, but he went on the offensive, slashing with the cutlass, drawing blood across one attacker's chest. Roland continued the movement, swinging the boarding axe. It knocked the club out of the second man's hands.

The second man got in a blow, missing Roland's head but hitting his shoulder with a solid strike. Roland ignored the pain and cut the man again with the cutlass across the back of the hand holding the club. It fell.

Both natives ran off, leaving their weapons.

Roland looked down the trail for anyone else.

"There were just two," the officer said. "Excellent job."

Roland turned. The officer hadn't offered any help during the brief combat, not that there'd been much opportunity. The images in the download strongly suggested that man was Captain Cook.

"What happened, sir?" Roland asked.

Cook cursed. "Fools. They stole my saber. When I demanded it back, they tried to kill me. We can't trust these savages. They'll steal anything that isn't secured. We will prepare a proper solution to this problem in the morning."

And then, not quite as quickly as he'd appeared, Captain Cook disappeared down the trail.

Roland remained where he was. Nothing about this in the download.

So.

The morning would be soon enough for him to die.

Roland didn't believe in easy, but maybe this mission was already over? He took the trail in the direction Cook had gone for lack of any other plan.

After a few minutes he came to a beach. There were two sailing ships at anchor in Kealakekua Bay: Cook's flagship the *Resolution* and the *HMS Discovery*. A boat was rowing out toward the *Resolution*.

Cook hadn't even bothered to wait for him.

Roland shrugged. Rank hath its privileges.

A noise to one side along the beach alerted Roland. He turned, reaching for his weapons. A beautiful young woman was walking toward him in the moonlight. She wore only a skirt, her perfect breasts coming directly at Roland, more deadly than many other weapons he'd faced.

Roland took a step back and looked from side to side, searching for an escape. He was on a rocky beach, waves crashing in on the right. Jungle to the left, quickly ascending to a ridge. There was the trail, but there were two bodies not far from it.

The woman was smiling and she stopped, gesturing with a hand for him to come to her.

Roland closed his eyes. "Neeley," he whispered, trying to get oriented.

It is 1779 A.D. Spanish troops take the town of Baton Rouge from the British; Tekle Giyorgis I starts his first of five terms as Emperor of Ethiopia; Francis Scott Keye is born; General 'Mad' Anthony Wayne takes Stony Point from the British; the Great Siege of Gibraltar begins and lasts over three years and at the end, the British are still there.

When Roland opened his eyes, the half-naked woman was still there.

Some things change; some don't.

Edith's download conveniently supplied the fact that the first Europeans to encounter the Hawaiians had been shocked at the sexual openness of the women. It seemed jealousy and possessiveness were a foreign concept in their society; which might also explain why they'd viewed Cook's sword as available.

Roland shook his head. "No, thanks."

But he had a moment of doubt, not lust. Was this woman also the mission?

He spun about as he heard voices behind him, but it was just another sailor, running after a native girl who was laughing. They dashed past without even acknowledging Roland and disappeared into the darkness down the beach.

The girl gestured again and said something in a language Roland didn't understand. But even Roland could decipher the implicit invitation in the tone and the way she stood.

He shook his head once more. "I've got a woman." He blushed, although it passed unseen. Calling Neeley his woman out loud didn't sound strange at all.

The situation was exacerbated when a second woman came out of the jungle and joined the first. They both gestured for him to go with them into the jungle.

Roland couldn't make out much detail in the dark, but there was no doubting both were beautiful, tall, and in excellent shape. The latter was something Roland could appreciate on various levels.

He looked over his shoulder. No one. This mission was shaping up to be the oddest yet, and that included battling Grendel in Heorot and being trapped in the Valley of Death at Gettysburg on the day after Pickett's Charge.

For some reason, Roland felt this was more dangerous than either of those.

"Who are you?" Roland demanded, wishing Edith had included the native tongue in the download.

The women looked at each other, then approached.

Roland took a step back, "Uh-uh," but he didn't bring up the axe or redraw the cutlass from his belt.

He was still trying to figure out a way to escape this female ambush, when one of the women spoke in perfect English: "You are an odd man, Roland."

"And, as if the Devil himself had decided their torments were insufficient, above the wind's howl and the inferno's roar came the interminable, agonized screams of the victims being roasted alive."

—Victor Gregg, survivor Dresden Firebombing

Dresden, Germany, 14 February 1945 A.D.

DOC WASN'T THERE, and then he was there, but he'd always sort of been there. It was the best way to explain how he arrived, becoming part of his current time and place without fanfare or excitement, which was irrelevant, since he was surrounded by frozen death. He was in the bubble of this day, not before, and hopefully he wouldn't be here afterward because without refrigeration, the rows and rows of slaughtered cattle on hooks would certainly begin to rot. And the power was going to fail very soon.

Doc knew that would pale in comparison with the odor of tens of thousands of humans burned up in the raid that was winging its way towards Dresden. He looked around a strung up carcass, searching for other POWs, but there was no one in sight. The slaughterhouse was lit by a few bulbs strung along electrical wires in the rafters.

Doc frowned. Something was wrong with that. Then he realized he was on the surface level of the slaughterhouse complex, where the meat was shipped. Safety from the coming raid lay in the storage below ground.

How much time did he have before the incendiary bombs began falling?

While the bubbles the Shadow punched in time lasted no more than 24 hours, they sometimes lasted less. It was dark outside, based on the lack of light along the edges of the blackout curtains lining the tall windows in the brick walls of the slaughterhouse. The fact the windows were intact was a testament to Dresden's exemption from previous bombing raids.

Where were the guards?

Doc cocked his head, listening. Voices. Speaking German. Doc crept among the dangling carcasses until he could see a large, open loading door. Several Germans, rifles slung, stood on the wooden dock, peering at the night sky.

There was the sound of an approaching aircraft, just one, its engines a faint drone. One of the soldiers put his rifle to his shoulder and made shooting noises, the others laughing.

A Christmas tree shaped green flare popped alight high in the sky.

The soldiers seemed puzzled, discussing what it could be.

Doc knew. Edith's download had all the deadly details. The flare was a Target Indicator, dropped by a twin-engined Mosquito marker plane. In the distance a red one ignited and then several more over the city.

It is 1945 A.D.. A German test pilot dies in the first vertical test flight of a manned rocket; Going My Way wins best picture at the Oscars; George S. Patton dies from injuries received in a car accident; Churchill resigns as Prime Minister after being defeated in the popular election; American troops occupy the southern part of Korea while Soviet troops occupy the northern part—this will have repercussions; Franklin D. Roosevelt dies; Ernie Pyle dies on Okinawa; the United States drops an atomic bomb on Hiroshima and 3 days later, another on Nagasaki; World War II officially ends on 1 September with the Japanese surrender in Tokyo Bay; the United States joins the United Nations; the Wilhelm Gustloff is torpedoed and sinks, killing an estimated 10,000 on board—the greatest loss of life in a single ship sinking; Eddie Slovak is executed for desertion, the first, and last, American soldier to be executed for this offense since the Civil War; Anne Frank dies; Oral penicillin is introduced; Werner Von Braun and other German rocket scientists surrender to the Americans; the Yalta Conference with Roosevelt, Stalin and Churchill; MacArthur returns to the Philippines; Five Grumman TBM Avengers in Flight 19 disappear on a training mission in what would be called the Bermuda Triangle; a group of Marines reach the top of Mount Suribachi and raise the U.S. flag.

From Edith's timetable, Doc knew he had twenty-three minutes before the first wave of heavy bombers started dropping their incendiary bombs and Dresden began to burn.

Some things change; some don't.

"Who are you?"

Doc spun about. A man wearing olive drab fatigues and a bedraggled field jacket was walking toward him.

"They call me Doc."

The man stopped, looking past, out the loading door and soldiers and then up into the sky. "What's that?"

"Target Indicator," Doc said. "And you are?"

"Sergeant Vonnegut." He looked at Doc. "You're different. Not like the others."

"What others?" Doc asked.

"The Angels who came to me."

Doc tensed. Valkyries, agents of the Shadow, were often taken as angels by people who met them.

"What did the Angels say?" Doc asked.

Vonnegut pointed toward the open door. "That they would come for me when the way was lighted."

As he tried to walk past, Doc put his arm out, blocking him. "Hold on. It's not safe out there."

"But the lights are here!"

Vonnegut was possessed, determined to go outside.

Between the guards and the bombers en-route, it was suicidal. Doc tackled Vonnegut, both of them tumbling to the slaughterhouse floor.

The sky lit up as the first pattern of incendiary bombs detonated. Mixed in were the heavy thuds and concussive waves of the 'cookies'; 4,000 pound high explosive bombs also known as blockbusters, designed to wipe out entire buildings and blow the windows and doors out of surrounding buildings, making them more susceptible to fire. These heavier bombs, Edith's download informed Doc as he struggled with Vonnegut, were also designed to take out water mains, hampering fire fighting. Cruelty layered on top of destruction.

None of this was in the immediate vicinity, but Doc knew the British, who bombed at night with their Lancasters, were just getting started. And once daylight came, the Americans would follow with their Flying Fortresses.

It was fortunate for Doc that Vonnegut had been a prisoner since the Battle of the Bulge the previous December, because he was weak from his meager POW diet.

Someone was yelling in German.

Doc looked up. One of the guards was pointing a rifle at the two of them, gesturing to move.

"We have to get underground," Doc yelled at Vonnegut, letting go of him and struggling to his feet. "This whole city is going to be an inferno!"

A blockbuster thundered nearby and the entire building shook.

Another guard was behind Vonnegut, unseen by the perhaps-future author. He raised his rifle in a way Doc had seen in the pits at Camp Mackall during training—to smash the butt of it into the back of Vonnegut's skull.

Doc rushed forward, shoving Vonnegut aside.

The last thing he saw was the butt of the rifle coming for his head.

And then darkness fell.

"Forget this world and all its troubles and if possible its multitudinous Charlatans—every thing in short but the enchantress of numbers." Charles Babbage reference the Countess of Lovelace, the first to create the first algorithm intended to be carried out by a machine. In 1840. Before the machine to use the algorithm had even been invented.

Philadelphia, Pennsylvania. 14 February 1946

MOMS WASN'T THERE, and then she was there, but she'd sort of always been there. It was the best way to explain how she arrived, becoming part of her current time and place without fanfare or excitement among those around her. She was in the bubble of this day, not before, and hopefully she wouldn't be here afterward.

There was also no fanfare because she was in a bathroom, standing in front of a cracked mirror. There was no one else in the room, which was easy to determine because the stalls had no doors on them. The bathroom was cold, drafty and one of the sinks kept up a steady drip that Moms instinctively knew couldn't be stopped.

Moms went to the door, creaked it open, and peered into the hallway. Also empty. She accessed the download for a schematic of the building in which ENIAC was housed and oriented herself. The woman's bathroom, the only one in the entire building, was, of course, the most remote. An afterthought in a previously all male domain.

Moms exited, went along the hall to a fire exit, and then descended a level to the main floor.

She pushed open a door and paused. The room in front of her was filled with the mainframe of a computer, which had less capacity than the pocket-sized satphone she'd left behind in the team locker room. The walls were lined with computer consoles, hundreds of cables looping along the front of them, dozens and dozens of white lights flickering.

It appeared to be chaos, but Moms knew from the download that making sense of that chaos was the work of the ENIAC six. A door swung open and a group of women walked in, one of them carrying a large cardboard box which she carried to a table in the middle of the room. She tipped it slightly and a slew of red and green Ping-Pong balls bounced out.

It is 1946. In a speech in Missouri, Winston Churchill mentions an Iron Curtain descending in Europe; the Japanese General who commanded the Death March is executed; Syria becomes independent of France; the first American V-2 is launched at White Sands; at Los Alamos, Louis Slotin receives a fatal dose of radiation from the Demon Core; a Jewish terrorist group bombs the King David Hotel in Jerusalem, killing 90, mostly British personnel; the first Tupperware is sold; in the last reported mass lynching in the United States two African-American couples are killed in Georgia; the first theme park opens in the United States, nine years before Disneyland, called Santa Claus Land; Indian Prime Minister Nehru asks the United States and Soviet Union to stop nuclear testing to save humanity—India would have its first bomb in 1974; Mensa is founded by two guys who think they're smart; Hermann Goring poisons himself two hours before his scheduled execution; a war starts in Vietnam between the Viet Minh and the French, which will end eight years later at Dien Bien Phu (at least for the French); Muslims and Hindus battle in the Week of the Long Knives in India leaving over 3,000 dead.

One of the women picked up a small white ball and threw it across the room. "If this is all he thinks we're good for, I say we quit." The ball bounced against one of the computer consoles, then back, rolling to a stop.

Some things change; some don't.

"I agree," one of the others said. "We keep talking and talking, but we have to make a stand."

The other women had knives and were slicing Ping-Pong balls in half.

"You can keep yapping or you can help," one of the slicers said. "Sooner we get this done, the sooner we get out of here. We have to be back early in the morning to get ready for the press. I'd like to get some shut-eye."

"It is what it is," another slicer said and Moms felt a pang at those words, used so easily to dismiss that which shouldn't be. "Nothing's changed and nothing is going to change."

Was this just about stopping the women from quitting? Moms wondered. The machine was going to be publicly displayed tomorrow, so they'd already done the work. The download informed her that the ENIAC Six were needed even after that, though. They were the only ones who could continue to program it and, more importantly, find and quickly repair one of the thousands of vacuum tubes, which burnt out on a regular basis.

The mystery of the sliced Ping-Pong balls was solved when one of the women who'd been complaining took several pieces over to one of the machines and glued a piece over one of the white lights.

"Just like those blinking lights in those terrible science fiction movies," the woman said, holding the piece in place, letting the glue dry. "Which of those brainiacs thought of this?"

"Someone in public affairs," another said. "Dog and pony show."

"Which are we?" another asked.

The half Ping-Pong cover made it look more, well, whatever. High speed for 1946. A task given to the women to do as if they were just secretaries rather than a key component of the entire operation. Moms stomped down on her Betty Friedan moment, given that *The Feminine Mystique* was still 17 years out, and focused on the here and now. Why was she here?

She remembered Scout's mission to UCLA in 1969, the evening the first Internet message was sent. The Shadow had sent two agents, a double-blind to trap Scout, but they'd also placed a bomb to blow up the lab.

Crude, but effective, if it had worked.

Moms checked the download, going over the schematic of the building. She grimaced as she remembered all the classes Mac had taught the team back at the Ranch outside Area 51 on explosives and how to emplace them in order to do the most damage. Mac was gone now, disappeared on the D-Day, 1944 mission. A troubled man, she hoped he had found some peace before the end, whatever that had been.

Moms went to the stairwell and went up to check the room above the main computer lab. A great place to emplace a shaped charge designed to explode downward, taking out whoever was in the room and the equipment.

She pushed open a door, entering a room with the same dimensions as the lab on the lower floor. It was full of discarded tables, desks, chairs, filing cabinets and other school debris. It was dim, just a few naked light bulbs casting shadows among the furniture. Moms wove her way through, checking left and right.

She wasn't overly surprised when she saw the bomb, a large steel box, approximately four feet to a side and two feet high, emplaced between two desks.

The red digital countdown read :30 and, as she watched, switched to :29.

'St. Valentine is the Patron Saint of affianced couples, bee keepers, engaged couples, epilepsy, fainting, greetings, happy marriages, love, lovers, plague, travellers, and young people. He is represented in pictures with birds and roses and his feast day is celebrated on February 14.'

Catholic Online

Italy, 14 February 278 A.D.

SCOUT WASN'T THERE, and then she was there, but she'd sort of always been there. It was the best way to explain how she arrived, becoming part of her current time and place without fanfare or excitement among those around her, which wasn't hard because she became aware of the here and now on a riverbank, underneath a bridge, foul-smelling water just a few feet away.

She was in the bubble of this day, not before, and hopefully she wouldn't be here afterward. Because it smelled bad and she knew they didn't have hot showers in 278 AD. She'd never truly appreciated the small things of daily living in her time until she'd traveled back.

She could hear people, the clatter of hooves on stones, the creak of wagon wheels moving.

The river was the Tiber and she was on the northern edge of the city, where the Via Flamina crossed. If it stunk this bad, she wondered what it was like downstream?

Scout knew she needed to go up there, find out what was happening, but she really didn't feel like it. History said someone would get beheaded today and she was here to make sure history was right. She didn't see any upside.

It is 278 A.D. Probus reorganizes defenses along the Rhine River after expelling the Franks from Gaul; Rome besieges Cremna; Maxentius, who would be Emperor of Rome one day, is born—he would die, here, at the Battle of the Milvian Bridge in 312; his body would be pulled from the river and his head cut off and displayed by Constantine.

"You're early."

Scout recognized the voice: Pandora.

Some things change; some don't.

Scout turned and faced the 'goddess'. "What do you want?"

Pandora stood next to the bridge's buttress, dressed in a green robe cinched at the waist with an ornate gold belt. She had a Naga staff in one hand: blade on one end, seven-headed snake pommel on the other. She was tall and thin, with thick black hair, divided by a single streak of white from above her left, straight back and ending behind her left shoulder.

"Is that any way to say hello to an old friend?" Pandora asked. "We last met, let me think, ah yes, in Greece. I forget the year."

"I doubt that," Scout said.

"Three-sixty-two BC," Pandora said, "or the more politically correct BCE."

Scout took a step toward her. "See? Why try to BS me?"

Pandora laughed. "Touché. Nice. But the important question isn't what I want, it's why are you here? Now? That's what I meant when I said that you're early. This place isn't important for another thirty-four years and in October."

Edith's download supplied the answer: The Battle of Milvian Bridge.

"This is where and when the bubble is," Scout said. "What are you doing here?"

"Trying to understand," Pandora said. "Why do you think *you're* here?"

"Saint Valentine," Scout said.

"*You* shouldn't be here and now," Pandora said.

Scout spread her hands. "It's a Shadow bubble. It's opening bubbles on other Fourteen Februaries. This is mine." Scout began to walk by Pandora to scramble up to the roadway to see what was happening, but Pandora put her free hand out and stopped her.

"This is wrong. You being here. Now. That's why I'm here. Saint Valentine? How could that cause a ripple, never mind a Cascade? There were several Valentines; even the Church named four. A myth coalesced through literature a millennium later."

Scout had begun to push against Pandora's arm, but she stopped. "So why am I here?"

"I can only deduce it's because the Shadow wants you here."

The Possibility Palace

Where? Can't Tell You. When? Can't Tell You.

In the spiraling labyrinth of the outer edge of the Pit of the Possibility Palace, Lara strolled downward, passing by the analysts sitting at their bland desks, studying scrolls and other documents. Most didn't spare her a glance.

Lara briefly wondered what kind of life they had outside of the Pit? Then wondered why she wondered. She didn't know who they were or where they came from. For that matter, she had no idea *when* they came from.

Of course, she knew that much, rather that little, about herself, so . . .

She stopped at a desk, where a small engraved wooden plaque proclaimed:

North America. 1929.

She stood there long enough for the old woman sitting at the desk to finally look up from a scroll she'd been perusing with all the attention of degenerate gambler at the next race's odds. The woman peered over a pair of reading glasses, irritated at the interruption.

"May I help you?"

"The Saint Valentines Day Massacre," Lara said.

"Yes?"

"One of my friends just went there."

"Oh!" The woman blinked furiously, as if the race had gone off and she'd missed the start. "You're one of them?" She lowered her voice at the question, looking left and right. "One of the Team?"

"Yes," Lara said. "How important are the men who get killed that day? What if they live?"

"Oh, we don't do that," the woman said, as if Lara had suggested they partake of some obscene sexual act. "As the administrator says, the vagaries of the variables make such a thing futile. Our century chief has her own saying: conjecture is confusing."

"Sure," Lara said. "Everybody's got a saying here."

"There's a reason for them, young lady."

Lara accepted the rebuke without comment. "Is there a timeline where the massacre didn't happen?" She indicated the scrolls. "Don't you compare data from various timelines?"

"Only ones we get reports on via the Space Between and—" the woman paused and looked about guiltily.

"I'm on the Team," Lara reminded her. "I have a need to know."

"From the refugees," the woman said. She indicated her fellow analysts. "We're mostly refugees from other timelines. From other times. I *lived* 1929 when I was in my thirties. But in my home timeline."

"What happened to it?" Lara asked. "Why did you have to leave? Did the Shadow destroy it?"

"I left in 1947, during the Second World War." She shook her head. "There was no end in sight, even though Berlin and Washington DC had been nuked. The Japanese were holding on to their Empire in the Pacific, including Hawaii, which they'd invaded on the 8th of December after destroying the American fleet. Europe was a wasteland. There was fighting still going on, but over scraps. As soon as either the U.S. or the Nazis managed to patch together a nuke, they used it. Not often, but often enough. The U.S. took out not just Berlin but also Hamburg. The Nazis used their second on Moscow and that got Stalin and his top people. The Russians essentially fell apart and out of the war. England shouldered on, but London was a ghost town as it was inevitable a V-3 with a nuke would hit as soon as the Germans put together their third bomb. People were laying bets on whether the US would take out Tokyo with some sort of replay of the failed Doolittle Raid strike or Paris, to wipe out Hitler and his top people since they'd relocated there, figuring it wouldn't get nuked. It was hopeless."

"Charming," Lara said. "What was different in your timeline to cause that divergence? From what's happened in this timeline? What did the Shadow do?"

The woman shook her head. "I don't know if the Shadow did anything to my timeline. We did most of it to ourselves. I've researched it. Believe me, I've gone over this timeline's history with a fine tooth comb to find the divergence spot. But there were many, going back centuries. Little things that were different in my history. I can't pinpoint just one. It was so similar, yet started going so different. I think the largest divergence was that the United States didn't enter

World War I. The war ended, but only after the Communists revolted in Germany, overthrew the Kaiser, and sued for peace. But Hitler was still Hitler. Instead of wiping out the Communists like he did in your timeline, he became one, eventually taking over the party. Then he invaded France. And betrayed Stalin. But some of the scientists stayed in Germany who fled in your timeline to the United States. Physicists who were communist." She sighed. "I could tell you many, many things that were different." The woman stood up and walked around her desk. She held out her hand. "I'm Beth."

"Lara."

Beth indicated the Pit. "Everything below us, in this timeline, is pretty much the same as my timeline."

"So the United States not fighting in World War I caused such a big change?"

Beth nodded. "You'd think all those lives saved, over one hundred thousand Americans died in your World War I, would be a good thing. But." She shrugged. "That's why we can't predict the future. Besides the fact we can't predict it," she added with a wry smile. "And it's why, as long as the present is stable, the past *must* stay intact. Why didn't the U.S. enter World War I in my timeline? A lot of small things adding up to a big thing. So it's our job to try to make sure all the things in this history, big and small, stay the same."

"Hold on," Lara said. "How old are you?"

"Sixty-one."

"The math doesn't add up," Lara said. "If you lived 1929 then you should be—"

"I came through the Space Between," Beth said, referring to the timeless area that was crisscrossed with Gates between timelines. "Somewhere in there I skipped a bunch of years. But I've been here for over thirty years since I came through."

"Did you have a Saint Valentines Day massacre in your timeline?" Lara asked.

"Yes. It happened the same. It's curious how one part of history, sociological, can be the same, while another part, political, can be so different. Of course, the delineation isn't clear cut. "

Lara put her hand on the wood railing that kept them from tumbling downward, into the past and most likely their death in the gray swirl below. She assumed there was a bottom, a physical one, since the Pit was real. But who knew?

"Your timeline didn't have a Time Patrol?"

Beth shook her head. "No. We just fumbled along. As I said, I'm not certain even now if the Shadow was attacking my timeline using Time Travel."

"So you don't know if the Shadow caused the Cascades? Or the ripples that caused the Cascades?"

"No," Beth said. "That's the strange thing. It could have just been the natural progression of my timeline. There was no overt attack by the Shadow that I was aware of. But, of course, there's so much I'm not aware of. That many of us aren't aware of."

"You got that right," Lara agreed.

"What I do know," Beth said, "is that it's gone now. Blacked out of existence in 1948. Something happened not long after I left. Something final. It's gone and everyone I knew is dead."

"I'm sorry," Lara said, knowing it was a vastly insufficient thing to say about an entire timeline of people that no longer existed.

"It's why we work so hard," Beth said. "We know what can happen."

Lara closed her eyes. "I can feel them. Hear faint voices."

"Who?" Beth asked.

Lara opened her eyes. "The billions of people who existed. Who lived this timeline to the present. They're out there. Part of history. Part of the fabric that makes the whole."

Beth nodded. "Sometimes I sense it. Almost hear it. Faint whispers. It makes me wonder."

"Wonder what?"

Beth pointed up. "Where this is all heading."

The Missions Phase II

"In this life all that I have is my word and my balls and I do not break them for nobody."

—Al Capone

Chicago, 14 February 1929 A.D.

"It's time," Strings said as a car drove past, then turned into an alley on the side of the S.M.C. Cartage Company and disappeared.

Ivar had actually been enjoying the breakfast; sausage patties and an omelet the waitress had recommended. And he knew Moran wasn't in the car, but that was as it was, is, supposed to be. Whatever. "All right. What now? Where's my police uniform?" he asked.

"Now we calls the other guys," Strings said. "Don't worry about no uniform." He indicated the plate. "You done?"

As if killing would wait on his breakfast, Ivar thought. Any delay and Moran might actually show up, but the download informed him that historically Moran had spotted the police car with the two mobsters dressed as cops idling a few blocks away and that was why he hadn't been one of the victims.

There was something wrong with that since the two other hitters they were supposed to meet were the guys with the Thompsons.

"Yeah," Ivar said, trying to make sense of the situation, but it wasn't making sense. *Welcome to time travel* he thought.

Strings went over to the phone and picked up the receiver. Ivar couldn't hear what he was saying from his position by the booth.

"You all finished, honey?" the waitress asked.

Ivar nodded, his focus on the garage across the street, his mind on possible ways this could end up going awry. Of course, he wasn't thrilled about the prospect about being in there when it happened as recorded by history.

"Don't go," the waitress whispered as she passed by him, taking his plate off the table.

Ivar was startled. "What?"

"Don't go over there," the waitress said, jerking her head toward the garage. "It's a bad place."

"Stop chatting with the old lady," Strings called from the phone. He hung up and gestured for the door. "Time to deliver our valentines."

The waitress pushed her way through a swinging door into the kitchen and Ivar paused, watching the door go back and forth, slower each time, feeling like he was the same, bouncing, slower and slower and . . .

The pressure of a gun muzzle against the back of his head got his attention.

"If I was gonna kill you, I'd have the string around your neck," Strings said. "There's some folks want to talk to you. So let's not keep 'em waiting."

"The only limit to our realization of tomorrow will be our doubts of today."
—President Franklin Roosevelt
The Great Bitter Lake, 14 February 1945 A.D.

"Berlin?"

Watson shrugged. "Germany first. That's always been the policy. We atomize the Nazis first when the bomb is ready."

Eagle relaxed slightly. The good news was that the war in Europe would be over before the A-Bomb was ready. The bad news was that getting Roosevelt to switch the target for the A-Bomb didn't appear to be his mission; it made sense that the first target planned would be in Europe. "And if the war is over with Germany? Then what?"

"Then the Japanese," Watson said, confirming history. "I tell you though. Between you and me, and I'm only telling you because you already know what's going to happen, Franklin doesn't want to use it at all. He doesn't trust the scientists. But, more than that, he sees beyond that first use. Uncorking the bottle as it were." Watson made a noise that sounded like a cough but might have been a chuckle. "Appropriate for where we are. Letting the genie out of the bottle. You can't put it back in."

Eagle knew it would be of some solace for both Watson and Roosevelt to know that those first two bombs would be the last two actually used—so far to Eagle's present. That the threat of nuclear weapons used in a mutually assured destruction scenario made even despots pause.

So far, Eagle reminded himself. In his last mission, Eagle had kept the Shadow from hijacking the largest nuclear weapon ever built, Tsar Bomba.

"Is that what you're here about?" Watson asked. "Should we tell the boys in Los Alamos to shut down?"

That gave Eagle pause. What if they did stop the Manhattan Project now? The Trinity Test was still some months off, to occur on 16 July. The test that Moms often claimed was the beginning of when it all changed, eventually leading to the opening of the first Rift. The Demon Core wouldn't even be created at the Hanford Site and shipped to Los Alamos for a while. And if there were no Demon Core, there would be no Rifts. And if there were no Rifts, there would be no Nightstalkers. And if there were no Nightstalkers, there wouldn't be the Time Patrol. And if--

Eagle's mind was racing, shifting lanes, drawing on his vast knowledge of history. Shut down Los Alamos? There would be no Hiroshima or Nagasaki explosions. But then the Japanese would most likely not capitulate and Operation Downfall, the invasion of mainland Japan, would go ahead with estimated casualties in the millions for both American and the Japanese. So many more than perished in those two blasts. And if—

But someone would invent the bomb. Eventually. And it might not be the USA. And if--

"You all right, son?" Watson asked.

Eagle blinked. Mission first. "Yes. I'm fine. No. I'm not here to get Los Alamos shut down."

"So they make the thing and it works?" Watson asked. "Because their record so far isn't so great."

"Is anything strange going on?" Eagle asked. "Do *you* have any idea why I'm here? Today? Did the old woman tell you anything about why I would be here?"

Watson shrugged. "The President is meeting with King Saud later today. But the heavy lifting was done at Yalta. They chopped up Europe for after the war. Lots of folks not happy about that, especially the Poles. But that's done and a small price for getting the Russians into the war in the Pacific. Stalin is back in Moscow. Churchill is heading home. We're only meeting this sandlot King because of the oil. The war is using a lot and we're going to need more than the U.S. can produce."

It was hard to believe that the United States had been an exporter of oil prior to and during World War II. In fact, part of the reason Japan had attacked Pearl Harbor in 1941 was a sanction on U.S. oil to the Japanese.

"But didn't you send some sort of message into the future?" Eagle asked. "An alert that something was off today?"

"If I sent it," Watson said, "wouldn't I send it in *my* future, *your* past? How would I know something is off, until it's off?"

The conundrum of past and future coming into the same moment. Watson only had six more days to get a message out. But if the message came as a result of this meeting, wasn't that a fundamentally flawed paradox? Unless Fate--

"But," Watson cut into Eagle's thoughts, "the President wants to meet you."

"What? Excuse me, sir, but the First Rule."

Watson nodded. "Yes, yes. He doesn't know you come from the future. He just knows you're, shall we say, different? Just as he knows I'm a little different." Watson put a hand on Eagle's shoulder. "He's sick, son. The least you can do is meet him. Maybe say what you can say. That things are going to turn out all right?"

What if they don't was Eagle's instinct, but he didn't voice it.

Watson, however, was ahead of him. "After all, you wouldn't be here if people weren't still around whenever you come from. So those A-Bomb boys don't blow up the world. There's some who are afraid that once they initiate that thing, they won't be able to stop it. And the whole world will explode."

Watson nudged Eagle down the passageway. "The old man is resting, waiting for the King to arrive. It will just be the three of us."

Eagle had met George Washington on the Ides mission and the nation's first President had been larger than life. The prospect of meeting the only four-term President of the United States was enticing. And he did have to get to the root of the mission.

And he knew he was equivocating, but he allowed Watson to lead him.

Watson stopped at a hatch. "Here." He turned the wheel.

Eagle felt that tingle, the one he'd experienced in combat.

Watson tried to push the hatch open. "Give me a hand, if you will?"

"What's going on?"

"You're meeting the President," Watson said.

Eagle felt something, but he wasn't certain what.

Watson sighed. "I'll go first. You can follow." He ducked his head and went through.

Eagle reluctantly, yet with anticipation, followed.

Franklin D. Roosevelt *was* inside. A porthole was open and an electric fan was making a futile attempt to move the sullen, hot air.

Roosevelt spoke as soon as Eagle was in. "You're a nervous fellow, aren't you?"

"Sir." Eagle wasn't sure what to do, snapping automatically to a position of attention.

Roosevelt was in a wheelchair, a blanket draped strategically across his lap, hiding most of the contraption. The random thought that it must be hot beneath that blanket crossed Eagle's mind.

"Relax, my friend," Roosevelt said, his voice edged with the timbre Eagle had listened to from recordings of the President's fireside chats. "I wanted to meet you because I needed to know if Oppenheimer's vision was correct."

"His vision, sir?" Eagle felt a chill at the mention of the physicist's name. Moms often quoted Oppenheimer's reciting of the Hindu poem after the Trinity Test: *I am become death, the destroyer of worlds.*

Roosevelt glanced at Watson, then back at Eagle. "This is all very strange to me. But there are many things that are strange to me. Seems more and more so every day." Roosevelt grimaced as he fidgeted in the chair. "My dear friend here—" he indicated Watson—"won't tell me his terrible secret. One that has afflicted him all his life. Something to do with you and some sort of secret, which I only become aware of when, apparently, I need to be aware of it."

"I'm not following, sir," Eagle said.

"I could ask how you got on board this ship since I've never seen you before," Roosevelt said. "And I have an eye for people. And the *Quincy*, mighty though she is, isn't that large. And, no insult intended, young man, just fact, you do stick out. But my dear friend asked me not to ask. So I will not ask." He sighed.

"I don't understand the science," Roosevelt said, "but a year ago Professor Oppenheimer called me in quite the panic. Told me that something had gotten out of control. *Going critical* was the term he used. And something weird happened and an angel—that's the word Oppenheimer used—an angel, appeared out of nowhere and told Op he could show him how to fix it, but only if a deal was struck. This Angel could direct Oppenheimer how to get the thing, a pile Oppenheimer called it, back under control. The deal was that when asked, I do as requested. That I give my word."

Eagle remained still, waiting.

"A great request, my word. But Oppenheimer said the fate of the world, the entire world, was at stake. He is not a man given to exaggeration, one of the reasons he got the job running Manhattan. The science part at least. So I gave it." Roosevelt spread his hands. "This, apparently, is the payback."

There was no record of any of this in the download or in all the history Eagle had read, including the classified material he'd had access to as a Nightstalker. No mention at all of the possibility of a pile going critical at any of the Manhattan Project facilities. It didn't happen. Whether because a Valkyrie intervened, which Eagle doubted, or because a Valkyrie started and stopped one, which he thought much more likely.

"Yes, I can see you are as confused as I am," Roosevelt said. "An Angel magically appearing. Fixing a problem even Oppenheimer and his whiz kids can't. Saving us from a major problem, based on what old Op said. Catastrophic, I believe was the exact word. And he's not the religious sort. Not in the least. Actually, his wife is a communist as are many of his associates. We had the damnedest time getting him a clearance."

"If I may ask," Eagle said. "When did this happen?"

Watson answered. "Interestingly enough, a year ago today."

Wrong year. Wrong place.

"This can't be," Eagle said. "The Shadow opens the bubble. This has to be the right year." He'd spoken out loud words that shouldn't have been uttered.

"'Shadow'?" Roosevelt repeated. "What's that?"

"Nothing, sir."

Watson spoke up. "It's part of this thing, sir. We can't talk about it."

Roosevelt shook his head. "Keeping a secret from the man who knows all the secrets. But you were right, my old friend. He's here, like you said he would be," Roosevelt said.

"This Angel, sir," Eagle said. "It's not an angel."

"Indeed?" Roosevelt didn't seem surprised in the slightest. "But whatever or whoever it was, it held up its end of the deal. Oppenheimer's problem, a dire one, was fixed. Oppenheimer told me that a great disaster was averted. From the words he chose and his demeanor, I have no doubt he was telling the truth."

"What's going to happen?" Eagle asked.

"I don't know," Roosevelt said. "That's the funny thing about the future. We don't know. We just make the best decisions we can with what we know and then muck about. I'm not the man I was. The man I *was*, many years ago, before my affliction, was full of himself. Certain of all the great things ahead in my future. I was taught a bitter lesson about anticipating the future."

Eagle tried to focus on what the President was saying, but his mind was reeling from the implications that this mission was off by a year. That the Shadow was manipulating things in a way that hadn't been foreseen and that Fate was also involved somehow.

"Then I was laid low," Roosevelt said. "1921. For a long time they didn't know what it was that took me down. But it was painful. Let me tell you that. People make much of the fact I can't walk, but they have no idea of the pain I went through. It was the pain that changed me, not the lack of use of my legs. It was so bad, there were times I desired death more than life. There is pain that terrible." Roosevelt peered at Eagle through his glasses. "I'm telling you this, son, because I don't know what awaits you. But know this. The pain. It made me a better man. A better President. It made me get out of myself. Understand others. Understand the less fortunate in life."

Roosevelt leaned back in his wheelchair.

For the first time, Eagle noted that the old man's hands were shaking. He shifted his focus to Watson. "Do you know what's going to happen, sir?"

"Just that the three of us are supposed to be here," Watson said. "In this cabin. The Angel told Oppenheimer that."

"What's odd," Roosevelt observed, "is that someone knew we'd be on this ship a year ago. Very strange, which is an understatement, since this meeting wasn't set until a few months ago. No one could have known we'd be here in his place. On board the *Quincy*. Rather specific. So maybe we shouldn't dismiss the concept of a higher power of some sort intervening."

The hair on the back of Eagle's neck tingled once more, stronger, a distinct feeling and he knew what was going to happen.

A Gate crackled into existence near the porthole.

"Time for you to go," Watson said.

"Where?" Eagle demanded.

Watson indicated he had no idea. "Wherever it leads."

Roosevelt was staring at the Gate. "What is it, Pa?" His use of his friend's nickname indicated how startled he was.

"A doorway," Watson said. "That's all I know."

"Curious," Roosevelt, master of under and over-statement, said.

Eagle stared at the President.

"I gave my word," the President said. "But that's not your word."

Eagle nodded. "It won't be Berlin," he said, then stepped through the Gate.

No kind deed has ever lacked its reward.

—Hawaiian Saying

Hawaii, 14 February 1779 A.D.

"Not to worry," the other half-naked woman said. "Captain Cook will still die when he is destined, after the sun comes up. As history records. You helped set that in motion by protecting him."

Another Time Patrol member might have considered the import of those words, but not Roland. He was focused on the immediate problem. His free hand drifted down to the hilt of the cutlass. "Who are you?"

"It should have been easy," the other woman said. "Seriously, Roland. Why couldn't you make this easy?" She indicated her body with both hands. "We had to go through all this and you still won't participate?"

Roland's hand tightened on the sword and he raised the boarding axe. "Who are you?"

"I'm Vesta," the first one said, "and this is Egeria. No man has ever been able to resist us."

Roland noted that both wore just the grass skirts and they weren't armed. At least not with the weapons Roland was used to facing: gun, claw, tooth, knife, bomb, etc.

"I don't think Ivar or Doc or even Eagle could have resisted us," Egeria said. She laughed. "Moms would have been interesting."

"You're not Gaia," Roland said. "Not with Pandora. You're with Diana. The bitch who shot at me with an arrow."

The two women looked at each other. "Impressive leap. Close but not quite right," Vesta said. "And we were told you might be a bit slow. Obviously, incorrect information."

"We weren't told you couldn't be seduced," Egeria said. "Who is Neeley? She must be someone very special."

"Why are you here?" Roland demanded, holding his ground as they took another step forward.

"We're here to take you on a journey," Egeria said. "Won't you come with us?"

"You're working for the Shadow," Roland said. "I'm not going anywhere with you."

"And it could have been fun," Vesta said. "You are quite the physical specimen. Neeley must enjoy you."

"Indeed," Egeria said. "This would not have been a burden at all if it had gone as planned."

"Initially planned," Vesta said. "But there are always backup plans."

Roland felt a sharp jab in his chest and looked down to see a small dart embedded in his skin, right in the V of the open shirt.

"What—" he began, but he was overwhelmed with a sudden wave of lethargy.

In his peripheral vision he saw a Gate coming into existence to his left.

As he went to his knees, and before he keeled forward unconscious, his last thought was he preferred HALOing in with weapon at the ready than this time travel crap.

And women--

"If I had to have the same thing again, I would do the same again, but I would hope I wouldn't have to."

—Air Marshall Arthur 'Bomber' Harris regarding the Dresden mission.

Dresden, Germany, 14 February 1945 A.D.

Doc came to consciousness in the midst of thunderous concussions.

Blockbusters he thought. Huge four thousand pound bombs going off. But what most awed him as he opened his eyes was the unearthly red glow. It wasn't just coming through the shattered windows of the slaughterhouse, it was also inside, part of the very air. The world was burning and Doc was in the middle of the inferno.

He sat up, head pounding from both the butt-stroke and the concussions of the bombs. He didn't see the guards or Vonnegut.

He had to get to the lower levels.

He scrambled to his feet, then staggered as a bomb blew in the wall behind the stairs, umbling debris down on.

Fire roared in through the opening, forcing Doc to retreat. He spun about, hoping to dash out hrough the loading dock. He felt the wind pulling him in that direction as a wall of fire filled the treet outside.

He saw a woman running, a child in her arms, just ahead of the firewall. The heat at the orward edge of the inferno caught the pair and they burst into flames, but she kept running for aalf a dozen strides before collapsing

It was an exit to hell.

Doc blinked, trying to see, as a black rectangle appeared between him and firestorm. Six feet igh, four wide.

A Gate.

He looked about, knew he had no choice, and ran for it.

"Sometimes it is the people no one can imagine anything of who do the things no one can imagine."

—Alan Turing

Philadelphia, Pennsylvania. 14 February 1946

Moms did a quick assessment—bomb, room, women and computer below, mission-- which ook four seconds.

:25

The bomb was steel cased, no seams she could see, and the digital display was buried under nick glass, which she had to assume, given the casing, was not easily breached.

She wrapped both arms around it and tried to lift, testing whether it was bolted in place.

The bomb moved, barely. Too heavy to pick up, but she could slide it.

A little.

:20

She struggled to move it once more and slid it about a foot and a half, before she had to stop or a moment.

She didn't have many moments.

:15

Not enough time to get it out of the room. Tip it and direct the charge away from the room below? She tried to get her fingers under the bottom edge. Strained to lift.

Not going to happen.

:10

A Gate crackled open to her immediate right. A black rectangle, so dark it absorbed light.

The Fates helping? The Shadow? Pandora?

:08

There was no more time. Moms took the only option, shoving the bomb into the Gate, but the darkness reached out, wrapping around not only the bomb, but her too, snapping her into the darkness.

"He saw with his own eyes the trophy of a cross of light in the heavens, above the sun, and bearing the inscription: Conquer By This."

-Eusebius: *The Life of Constantine* just before the Battle of the Milvian Bridge

Italy, 14 February 278 A.D.

"Why?" Scout demanded.

Pandora shrugged. "I don't pretend to understand the Shadow's motives other than it is evil and destroys all it touches."

"So you're here to help me?" Scout asked, looking about, half-expecting Legion assassins to come rushing forward. It wouldn't be the first time. Or the second. Or the third.

"I'm here to find out what the Shadow has planned," Pandora said.

"Gee, thanks," Scout said. "Could I borrow your Naga?" she indicated the bladed staff.

"Not likely," Pandora said.

"You're not much help."

"Join me and I will be of tremendous help," Pandora said. "Be with us. The sisterhood."

"Of Gaia?"

"Yes."

"Not today," Scout said, still looking out for an ambush. "After all, you said I shouldn't be here. Now. Today. So not today."

"Too bad," Pandora said. "Then I'm done here."

"You're an ass," Scout said. "Not the best recruiting tool."

"You're not as smart as I thought you were," Pandora said. "And perhaps not as gifted with the Sight."

"Yeah, yeah," Scout said. "You've been blathering that since I first met you in Greece. How did the Alexander the Great thing turn out? Like you envisioned? With your Sight?"

"You're also not as funny as you like to think you are," Pandora said.

"He wasn't the 'One' was he?" Scout said. "You're not as smart as you think you are."

"Join us."

"Moms got me my high school diploma," Scout said.

"What?"

"She thought of me," Scout said. "She takes care of me. And the rest of the team. Do you take care of your people like that?"

"You don't know me and you don't know what you're really up against," Pandora said.

"You keep telling me I don't know stuff," Scout said, "but you never tell me what I don't know."

Pandora turned, as if listening to the bustle of traffic on the bridge above. The creak of poorly lubricated wagon wheels, the clatter of horse's hooves on stone, muted voices. "Oh," she murmured.

"What?" Scout said.

"Fate."

"Where?" Scout asked, trying to focus, to project her Sight.

Pandora shook her head. "So what will be, will be. That is what Fate decrees." A Gate opened behind her and she stepped backward and was gone.

"Great," Scout muttered. First Pandora with her usual vague warnings and now a Fate around. Somewhere.

Scout wasn't picking up anything extraordinary, but she didn't exactly know what she was supposed to pick up from a Fate since only some of her teammates had encountered one on a mission. No one even knew who or what they were. But if it scared Pandora off—that wasn't good. Then again, maybe it was? Based on the debriefs, interventions by Fates were usually on the side of the Patrol, not the Shadow.

Scout scrambled up the steep slope of the Tiber embankment, narrowly avoiding a stream of urine from a man standing on the edge of the road. He didn't seem embarrassed or concerned about the near miss.

When in Rome.

Scout got to the level of the road. The traffic was heavy as the Via Flaminia is the major road running north out of Rome and over the Apennine Mountains to the northeast coast of Italy. Edith's download threatened to deluge Scout with information about the road, how it was built, who traveled on it and much more. Apparently, Edith had a thing for Roman construction. Scout was impressed with how smooth the road was and how tightly packed the stones; in better shape than many modern roads.

Scout shut that down and focused on the people, not so much what she was seeing and hearing, but the flow of the world around her; the stream of humanity. Mostly exhaustion from those trudging along, which appeared to her as a dull purple. Some flickering red as a cohort of soldiers tramped by heading north, their leather sandals a rhythmic slap against the flat, closely joined stones.

Lots of knee problems later in life for them, Scout thought, but she also knew the average life span wasn't long enough to worry about bad knees in your 60s. And legionnaires had a shorter life span than most.

There was the slightly brighter glow from merchants heading south with their wagons. The expectation of making money. Of a good deal. Some of their auras were darker, fear of a bad deal. Worry was a pervasive emotion among almost everyone. Worry about this or that.

The human condition.

It exhausted Scout, but not as much as the darkest auras: The dull gray, rippled with black, of slaves passing by, nothing but despair filling their lives.

She picked up something different, vibrant, passionate. An old man in a red robe was coming across the bridge. People were parting for him, actually, not him but because right behind him strode an imperious man in a white robe fringed with purple who was escorted by a dozen tough-looking legionnaires. The man in the red robe had a fringe of white hair around his skull and his skin was deeply tanned and wrinkled.

He stopped at the midpoint of the bridge, next to a beggar who was seated with his back against the waist-high stone wall that bordered the roadway. The beggar had a wooden bowl in front of him and a dirty rag tied around his head, covering his eyes.

The old man looked about, inspecting the people passing by. The other man and his guards also stopped, waiting.

The old man, whom Scout assumed was Valentine, eventually to be Saint Valentine, leaned over and said something to the beggar. It seemed the beggar was blind, although the random thought crossed Scout's mind that Nada might not have so easily believed that, putting the man to some sort of test.

Nada had been a bit cynical.

Valentine straightened and look around. His gaze paused on Scout. He smiled at her and she felt drawn in by his amazingly blue eyes, and was also unsettled that he'd noted her. But he looked past her and the smile disappeared.

Scout looked over her shoulder.

Fate.

An old woman in a white robe, a rod held in one hand across her body, the length of it in the crook of the other arm. Edith's download kindly informed Scout the woman matched the description of Lachesis, the middle of the three Fates. The disposer of lots; the one who determined how long the thread of life that Clotho spun would last. The rod was to measure life. But she ruled not only the length of life, but also a person's destiny. No one on the team had reported seeing Lachesis before: Clotho and Atropos, the spinner and cutter, but not her, the apportioner.

"Lucky me," Scout muttered. Another first for her. It also appeared as if no one but her and Valentine saw the Fate.

"Do you wish to see?" Valentine's voice was surprisingly loud and caught the attention of many on the bridge. A merchant halted his wagon, causing a minor traffic-jam when combined with the other man his military contingent.

"Do you wish to see?" Valentine said once more.

The beggar was nodding.

"Duh," Scout muttered. She was leaning toward Nada-land, that perhaps this was an elaborate con, set up by Valentine and the beggar. Glancing over her shoulder, she noted that

Lachesis hadn't moved, the rod in the crook of her arm, the hood of her white robe covering most of her face.

Valentine turned to the crowd. He pointed at the man in a fine robe, flanked by the legionnaires. "Judge Asterius has promised me freedom if I can show him the power of my faith and belief in the one true God. We have agreed that if I can make a blind man see, that will be sufficient."

The Judge raised a hand, stopping Valentine. He gestured at one of his soldiers. The legionnaire drew his sword, walked up the beggar. He ripped the rag off the beggar's head, and then slashed at him, halting just an inch from the man's face.

The beggar never flinched or showed any awareness of the near strike.

Apparently Judge Asterius was of the Nada/Scout bent in terms of trust, or lack thereof.

Valentine gave the Judge a tolerant smile. "Satisfied?"

Asterius shrugged, his level of enthusiasm muted, to say the least.

A large crowd had gathered on the Malvian Bridge, caused as much by the traffic jam as the miracle in the making.

Scout checked Lachesis once more. She hadn't moved.

The download was confirming some of what she was seeing: one legend about St. Valentine was he had been arrested by a Judge Asterius, but that he'd then preached Christianity to the Roman official. Asterius had made a deal: if Valentine could restore his adopted daughter's sight, he would be freed and Asterius would convert.

This was a bit different, beggar not daughter, but the names were right. Except today was the day Valentine was supposed to die, not be freed from prison.

Scout recalled Dane's favorite sayings: The vagaries of the variables.

Valentine put his hands over the beggar's eyes.

Sensing something with the Sight, Scout turned. Lachesis was moving forward, seeming to slide along the ground in her robe rather than walk. She stopped next to Scout, almost touching. She extended her rod toward Valentine and the beggar.

"In the name and strength of my Lord," Valentine called out, "you will now see!"

Valentine removed his hands and the beggar staggered to his feet, blinking.

"Do you see, my brother?"

The beggar cried out: "No! I can't."

"Uh-oh," Scout muttered.

Valentine spun about, pointing. "It was her! The witch!"

Scout looked to her right, but Lachesis was gone. The crowd was staring at Scout.

"Crap," Scout muttered.

Asterius showed why he was a judge, gesturing toward the same legionnaire who'd tested the beggar. His sword was still drawn and he didn't hesitate, swinging hard, separating Valentine's head from his body with a single blow. The head arced into the air, tumbling, and disappeared over the side of the bridge.

Then Asterius pointed at Scout. "Her too."

Scout took a step back as a half dozen of Asterius's guards pushed through the crowd toward her, weapons drawn. She took another step in retreat, her back against the wall of the bridge. She glanced over her shoulder. The Tiber was sluggishly flowing forty feet below.

Valentine was dead, beheaded, on this day as history decreed. Scout didn't see any point in sticking around and adding a footnote to that history. She scrambled up onto the stone wall and dove.

She saw the Gate open between her and the water the split second before she would have hit the surface.

The Possibility Palace

Where? Can't Tell You. When? Can't Tell You.

Lara walked into Dane's office without knocking. "Something's wrong."

Dane wasn't perturbed or surprised. "Something is always wrong. That's why we exist."

Lara sat down across from him. "This mission. Something's not right about it. You knew it in the briefing. That's why you were acting wonky."

"'Wonky'?"

"Can we cut the back and forth like you do with Scout?" Lara asked.

"All right."

"Why didn't you send me on a mission?" Lara demanded.

"Because of what you just said," Dane replied. "Something's off. The letter from Meyer Lansky for one. Ivar was right. That's just weird. Sometimes things loop. We had one between Doc and Moms' mission on Independence Day."

"They told me about that," Lara said. "That was quick thinking on Doc's part."

"There's something about it that bothers me," Dane said. "Once the Shadow's bubble collapses, what happened inside that bubble is gone. Things go on as they did in history. But Jefferson remembered what Doc told him about a woman coming to him at Monticello."

"And Benjamin Franklin remembered Doc from the Independence Day mission during the Nine Eleven mission."

"You pay attention," Dane said. "That's good."

Lara didn't respond to the praise.

"Ivar violated the rules when he met Meyer Lansky," Dane said. "He didn't have much choice since we'd made a mistake and gave him thousand dollar bills printed *after* his mission date. A bad mistake, especially with someone as sharp as Lansky. As improbable as the concept of time travel is, Lansky knew something was, as you say, wonky. There's a reason he never got assassinated—he was a brilliant man. A psychopathic criminal, but brilliant."

"Perhaps Ivar telling Lansky punctured the bubble somehow," Lara said. "Same with Doc telling Jefferson about Moms being there fifty later at Monticello. Just enough to make the loops and it lasted after the bubble collapsed?"

"Perhaps," Dane allowed.

"So do you know what the problem with this mission is?" Lara asked.

"No."

"You still haven't answered why you didn't send me on one of the missions," Lara said. "What good does it do for me to be here?"

"You're the wild card," Dane said. "What you did to fix the ripple from Scout's mission regarding Pythagoras was—" he paused—"something I don't understand but it helped."

"I don't understand it either," Lara said. "You want me to go to the Space Between again? Hook up with Amelia Earhart? Go to the Atlantean ship?"

Dane shrugged. "We don't know what's wrong, so how can we know how to fix it? Maybe everything's going fine on the missions."

"It's not," Lara said. "When I affected Scout's mission with Pythagoras, I had part of his sculpture to make a physical connection with that time and place. We don't know what I'm supposed to do in this case."

"What are you picking up?" Dane asked.

"Voices in the Pit," Lara said. "There's billions of them; all of the people who've lived and died."

"One hundred and seven billion is the best guess," Dane said. "The number of humans who have existed. It's a rough estimate because we don't know when our species specifically became human from what we were before. Nevertheless, that's a lot of voices."

"Yes, but—" she paused.

"What?"

"There are some voices I can pull out of the torrent," Lara said. "Team members. Not speaking. Singing."

"Who is singing?" Dane asked. "Which team members?"

Lara closed her eyes. "Scout. I can hear Scout." Her voice dropped to a whisper. *"Shadows are fallin' and I'm runnin' out of breath. Keep me in your heart for a while."* Her eyes opened, glistening. "So sad. She's so sad."

"That was her song with Nada," Dane said. "The former team sergeant."

"Eagle said he made the choice to go back, when you gave it to him."

"I didn't give it to him," Dane said. "Sin Fen did. But, yes, he chose to go back and change something. To right a wrong."

"I thought we weren't supposed to do that," Lara said. "Rules and all."

"There are exceptions to every rule," Dane said.

"Surprised you'd admit that."

"And it is a true choice. An important one."

"Okay," Lara said.

"Who else do you hear?" Dane asked.

"Doc."

"Is he also singing Warren Zevon? The team uses Zevon songs for different things."

Lara shook her head. "Not a Zevon song. Dylan. *Knockin' on Heaven's Door.*" She was surprised. "How did I know that was a Dylan tune?"

"Zevon did a cover of it," Dane said. "I had to study up."

"I don't think that's a good song," Lara said. "Neither of them."

"Anyone else?"

"No. But those two are bad enough. Sadness and despair." She stood. "Time for me to get closer to the team."

The Missions Phase III

"Hell must be a pretty swell spot, because the guys that invented religion have sure been trying hard to keep everybody else out."

—Al Capone

Chicago, 14 February 1929 A.D.

Strings shoved Ivar into the back of a large, black sedan and slid in next to him, pushing him toward someone. And against the snout of a Thompson submachine gun that the guy had across his lap.

"Watch it," the man said.

"Sorry," Ivar said, his usual response when bumping up against an automatic weapon held by a man with dead eyes.

There was another man in the driver's seat, slouched back, brim of his hat tipped down over his face. The muzzle of a Thompson stuck up next to him. The driver briefly lifted the brim of the hat and glanced in the rear-view mirror. Judging by how blood-shot they were, the driver wasn't having a good morning.

Join the club, Ivar thought. But did not say.

"Who's this?" the guy next to Ivar asked.

"Told ya about him, Sam," Strings said. "He's part of the deal. Capone wants him in."

Ivar looked out the window and saw the old waitress at the window of the café, staring at him. She raised a hand and gave a wave, along with a sad smile.

She knew, Ivar thought. Which begged the question: *how?* Which brought up the further question: *Knew what?*

The driver asked: "Why?" His eyes were open all the way and he sat up straighter. "Al's in Florida. He didn't tell me nothing about no extra gun. When did you talk to him?"

Strings leaned over and extracted Ivar's .45 from the holster. "He aint an extra gun."

Just like that, his weapon was gone. Ivar could well imagine Roland's reaction, but Roland wasn't here and he was and there was an automatic weapon pointed in this direction.

"Then what's he doing here?" the driver asked.

"You'll see, Tony," Strings said.

Tony wasn't buying it. He shifted his questioning to the guy on the other side of Ivar. "You hear anything about this, Sam?"

Ivar was checking Edith's download: Tony and Sam. The most likely results were discouraging: Tony Accardo, aka Joe Batters or the Big Tuna, and Sam Giancana. They were rumored to have been in on the massacre and both went on to play large roles in the mob, with Accardo ruling the Chicago Outfit starting in 1947 and Giancana taking over for Accardo in 1957.

Where were the two fake policemen? Ivar wondered. More importantly: *why was he here?*

And most importantly: *given his present company, and the way they didn't seem to think he was on their side, was he going to be alive when this bubble collapsed?*

*****

EAGLE WASN'T THERE, and then he was there. It was the best way to explain how he arrived, becoming part of his current time and place with an appropriate degree of surprise and excitement on everyone's part, including Eagle's, as he suddenly appeared inside the S.M.C Cartage Garage via the Gate.

Two men, one in a cheap suit wearing a fedora, the other in an expensive suit and no hat, reacted quickly despite their shock, drawing pistols from shoulder holsters and training them on Eagle.

"Who the hell are you?" Expensive Suit demanded. "Where'd you come from? What is that thing?"

The Gate snapped shut behind Eagle.

An old truck up on jacks was to one side, and an old car to the other (old being relative, since the car was spotless and probably new). A mechanic in coveralls and dirty white t-shirt slid out from under the car to see what was happening. The garage had brick walls and a workbench littered with tools. A table was in a corner with several chairs around it, where the two men in suits had been sitting. A desk was outside a door with opaque glass that read 'PRIVATE'. One wall had a large metal sliding door. A German Shepherd was whining, hiding underneath the truck, tied by a rope to the bumper.

Between the car, the truck, the way the two men were dressed, the mechanic and the garage, Eagle didn't have to make much of a leap to figure out when and where he was.

He just didn't understand *why*.

And he didn't see Ivar.

The two men walked over, guns at the ready.

"Hey!" Expensive Suit yelled. "I'm talking to you, spook."

Spook? Eagle was surprised by the term, but that was interrupted when the muzzle of the man's pistol swung toward his head.

Eagle instinctively blocked it with an arm sweep, but didn't follow through as the other man ordered: "Freeze or I'll blow your brains out!"

Expensive Suit took a step back, looking Eagle up and down. "He's a Navy boy, Goosey. How did you get in here? What do ya want?"

Eagle desired the answers just as much.

Goosey spoke "He just stepped out of nothing."

"Nobody comes from nothing," Suit said. "He came through that black thing. Like a door 'cept it's gone now. He snuck in here to steal something." He waggled his gun. "You picked the wrong place, buddy. You know who I am?" He didn't wait for an answer. "I'm Jim Clark."

Eagle accessed the backup information on Ivar's mission. Jim Clark, born Albert Kachellek, and Bugs Moran's right hand. The man whose death would haunt Al Capone's dreams.

That confirmed time and place for Eagle. Chicago, 1929, which meant somehow he was indeed in Ivar's mission. Except no Ivar. Which meant—

Eagle's thoughts were interrupted as Clark gestured toward a nearby wooden chair. "Sit down, boy."

With two guns trained on him, Eagle sat.

"Hands behind your back."

Eagle complied and Goosey, whom the download identified as Peter Gusenberg, an enforcer for the Moran gang, went behind him and used a piece of cable to tie his hands behind his back. The mechanic, sitting next to the car, saying nothing, watching with wide, scared eyes, was John May.

Eagle wondered what time it was, because at 10:30 there were going to be a lot of bullets flying in here and these three men would be dead. But there was supposed to be seven.

Which also meant--

There was a crackling sound and everyone looked toward the same spot where Eagle had just appeared.

*****

ROLAND wasn't there, and then he was there. Roland tumbled through the Gate onto the floor.

Out like the proverbial light. Switched off. Unconscious.

Goosey and Clark looked at each other, then at the large man dressed in tight white, cut off pants, unbuttoned calico shirt and with a cutlass in a leather waistband and a boarding axe loosely grasped in one hand.

Roland could still hold on to his weapon even when not conscious.

"What the hell is going on?" Goosey demanded. "Where are these guys coming from?"

"Shut up," Clark said. "It's some sort of magic thing maybe. Someone's screwing with us. Come on." He leaned over and pulled the cutlass out of Roland's waistband and relieved him of the boarding axe. "There's blood on these," he added. "This guy's a fighter. Look at the scars."

"You think Capone sent him?" Goosey asked as the two struggled to drag Roland over to the chair next to Eagle.

"Just be glad he was out," Clark said. "He looks like he coulda made a ruckus."

They were unable to lift Roland up and keep him in the chair so they improvised by tipping the chair over and using some rope to tie Roland in a sitting position on his left side.

Clark went to Eagle and jammed the muzzle of his pistol into the soft spot under his chin. "Who are you guys? Who you working for? How are you just appearing out of nothing? You know this guy?"

Even if he wanted to, Eagle couldn't have responded with the gun shoving his head back.

It didn't matter, though, as there was another crackling sound.

Clark pulled the gun away and turned about.

*****

DOC WASN'T THERE, and then he was there. He came through the Gate cowering, with his arms over his head in a protective posture.

Doc was motionless for several moments, then he slowly straightened and lowered his arms. His initial feeling was one of immense relief not to be in the midst the Dresden firebombing. He took in the two men with guns trained on him, Eagle in the chair, Roland, unconscious, on the floor and his relief began to fade.

"What the devil?" Doc said.

"Shut up," Clark said.

"Eagle?" Doc asked, confusion slowly giving way to awareness.

"No clue," Eagle said.

"Where's—" Doc began, but Eagle cut him off.

"Roland's right there. He's breathing, so that's good."

Doc could only nod as Clark forced him down into a chair and tied him.

"So you guys do know each other," Clark said, stepping back to survey the three of them. "Who you with? Capone? How you getting in here?" He looked over at the mechanic. "You know these guys?"

John May shook his head. "No, sir. Never seen 'em before in my life. I swear."

The door near the desk swung open and two men dressed in black overcoats walked in, pausing just inside the garage, taking in the strange scene.

"What's going on, Jimmy?" one asked Clark. "Who are these people?"

"Don't know. They just showed up."

"What do you mean 'just showed up'?" the same man asked.

"Heyer, you know as much as I know, okay?" Clark said.

That identified him as Adam Heyer, the bookkeeper for the Moran gang. A process of elimination and mug shot photos in the download, tabbed the other man as Reinhardt Schwimmer. Technically not a member of Moran's gang, but more a hanger-on; a former optician who liked associating with gang members and was, in the download's terms, a degenerate gambler.

They were both supposed to die this morning.

"Call Moran," Clark ordered Goosey. "Tell him something really weird is going on."

"He's probably already on the way," Goosey argued.

"Do it."

Goosey had just lifted the receiver on the phone on the wall next to the desk when the Gate opened once more.

*****

Moms wasn't there, and then she was there, along with the bomb.

"It's live!" she yelled as it thudded to the floor and she landed on her knees next to it. She was so focused on the device, she didn't notice anything else as the digital countdown clicked to:

:05

And stopped.

Moms watched for a couple of seconds to ensure that the timer had halted, then her training kicked in and she rolled, underneath Clark's gun, knocking it to the side with one arm while striking him directly in the groin with her other fist.

As Clark doubled over she grabbed for his pistol.

The bullet from Goosey's gun hit her before she could get the weapon.

*****

Scout wasn't there, but then she was there, still falling, just in time to see Moms shot. Then Scout hit the greasy floor of the garage with a solid thud that knocked the breath out of her.

*****

The Time Patrol was in the bubble of this day, not before, and hopefully they wouldn't be here afterward.

But it wasn't looking good at this moment in time.

The Space Between

"Ever think of putting together some sort of landing pad?" Lara asked as water dripped from her grey, Time Patrol issue coverall and the Gate closed behind her.

"Valkyries come by here occasionally," Amelia Earhart said. "Any sort of platform would draw attention. You don't want them waiting to meet you." On the sandy shoreline behind her, a half-dozen Samurai were arrayed, facing outward, providing security. Earhart appeared to have aged only slightly from the last photos taken of her before she disappeared on her round-the-world flight. In whatever timeline she came from.

Lara wrinkled her nose at the thick, oily odor that permeated the air. "Still stinks."

"Nothing much changes here," Earhart said.

Lara had arrived through a Gate to a point offshore, just above the water. Splashed in and swam to shore. The large, dark lake in the center of the Space Between extended behind her as far as one could see. Overhead, a gray mist blocked whatever was above. The shore was composed of a black, sand-like substance.

Within sight were over a dozen black columns extending from the surface of the water upward to the haze. Gates and Portals between worlds and times. The shoreline was dotted with ships and planes, vanished from their Earth timeline and stranded here.

Lara asked the obvious question. "How did you know I was coming?"

Earhart pointed clockwise along the beach. "We didn't. That appeared not long ago. We've been observing it."

A column, rippling with gold and blue, flickered over the edge of the water a quarter mile away. It was just offshore of the *Cyclops*, a ship that had disappeared in the Bermuda Triangle in 1918.

"Ever see a column like that before?" Lara asked.

"No," Earhart said. "Which is why we've been observing it. We don't know what it means. But the fact you're here indicates something strange is going on. Correct?"

"Yeah," Lara said, staring at the column. "No idea what it's connecting? What worlds or times?"

"No," Earhart said. "We see flickers of gold or blue in Gate columns sometimes. But nothing this extensive."

"Let's check it out."

The Mission Phase IV

"I'm a kind person. I'm kind to everyone, but if you are unkind to me, then kindness is not what
you will remember me for."

—Al Capone

Chicago, 14 February 1929 A.D.

Clark had his gun against Moms' temple, finger twitching on the trigger. "I oughta kill you, bitch." He was breathing hard from the brief fight and the blow to the balls.

Blood was pooling underneath Moms' right leg. She barely noticed the wound, taking in the rest of her team, minus Ivar, in the garage.

"How's Roland?" she asked Eagle.

"Breathing," Eagle said. "There's a small dart in his chest. Looks like someone drugged him. No obvious damage."

Clark shoved the muzzle of his pistol against Moms' temple. Hard. "I'm talking to you lady."

"I hear you," Moms said.

"I oughta—" Clark began.

"Please don't," Eagle called out. "We'll tell you what's going on."

Clark, Goosey and company, and the rest of the Time Patrol focused on Eagle, because they *all* wanted answers.

"You're going to die this morning," Eagle said.

Clark pulled the gun back from Moms' head, but still kept it aimed at her. "What?"

"Capone has put a hit out on Moran and his crew," Eagle said. "This meeting is a set up."

"Capone's in Florida," Goosey said.

"That don't mean he can't put a contract out," Clark said. "Keep the other dame covered," he ordered as Scout sat up, trying to get oriented.

"Dame?" Scout muttered.

"What is this?" Clark asked, indicating the bomb.

"Can we care for her wound?" Eagle nodded toward Moms.

Clark ignored Eagle for the moment. "You packing?" he asked Heyer and Schwimmer.

"I do the books." Heyer was shaking his head.

Schwimmer pulled a snub nose revolver out of the pocket of his coat. "I got this."

With a look of disgust, Clark went to a locker and opened it. Inside were several double-barreled shotguns. "Grab a scattergun," he yelled to the mechanic. "You guys too," he indicated both Schwimmer and Heyer.

"Hold on!" the mechanic protested. "I just fix the trucks and cars. I aint—" he paused, regrouping. "I don't get paid to hold a gun," he ended weakly. He walked over and grabbed one of the shotguns.

Schwimmer and Heyer also took a shotgun. While Goosey kept the Team covered, Clark made sure each of them had rounds in the chambers.

"You just aim and pull the trigger," he told them. "Any of them causes trouble, you give it to em. Both barrels."

The trio didn't look comfortable with the thought, but the glint in Clark's eyes negated any thought of arguing.

Moms pressed down on her leg to stop the bleeding. She was still sitting on the floor and twisted, pulling up her long skirt, looking for an exit wound to match the dark hole in the right front of her thigh.

Clark turned his attention to the team. "You," he said to Scout. "Get next to her."

Scout scooted over on the floor to Moms.

"Who are you people?" Clark asked. "You all know each other?"

"We're friends," Eagle said.

"Shut up spook," Clark said. "Who's in charge? The big lug there?" he indicated Roland.

"Not," Scout said.

"I am," Moms said.

"A dame?" Clark wasn't buying it.

Moms grimaced as she found the exit wound. "Clean through and through," she updated Eagle. "Full metal jacket. No bone. No artery. Pretty lucky." She began ripping strips off the hem of her dress.

"You talk to me!" Clark yelled. "You people appear out of nowhere and tell us Capone's put a hit on us for today. I'm gonna start shooting until I get some answers that make sense. And what is this thing?" he indicated the bomb once more.

Moms stuffed a piece of cloth into the exit wound. She looped a strip around her leg and cinched it tight, a tremor the only sign of pain. "If you shoot us, then you have no one who can answer your questions."

"I can shoot one or two of you to get the others to answer," Clark pointed out.

"But you don't know which of us have the answers you want," Moms said.

Clark indicated Roland. "He aint talking anyway, so we won't miss him." He walked over and stood above the big man, weapon pointed. "Someone gonna start talking?"

"That thing is a bomb," Moms said. "It has a timer that's stopped at five seconds."

Clark frowned. "Never seen a bomb like that before." He went over and looked at the display. "Yeah, it reads five." He shifted his attention. "Why are those guys dressed up like sailors?" He indicated Roland and Eagle. Then Doc. "And the flyboy? And what's with her?" he pointed at Scout, in her Roman rags.

"You're James Clark," Moms said. "Your real name is Albert Kachellek. But you changed it so your mother wouldn't be embarrassed because of your criminal lifestyle. You have the tattoo of a naked woman on your left forearm."

Clark was very still. "How do you know about that?"

"It's written in your autopsy report," Moms said.

"My what?"

"The coroner noted it in his report," Moms said. "He'll be writing it tomorrow."

Clark was blinking fast, confused. "What?"

"Where are the others?" Moms asked.

Clark glanced at Goosey. "What others?"

Moms lifted a bloodied hand. "You. You. You." She indicated the mechanic, Heyer and Weinshank. "That's five. Seven of you get killed in here today. Machinegunned by Capone's people."

A voice called out from the back door to the garage. "But there's ten of you in here. Plenty to kill."

Sam Giancana followed up his statement with a short burst from his Thompson, the roar of the gun echoing in the garage. The big .45 caliber bullets hit Goosey, sending him flying.

"Drop it," Accardo advised Clark, the muzzle of his Thompson emphasizing the order. He was shoulder-to-shoulder with Giancana, packing enough firepower to wipe everyone out.

Clark looked at May, Heyer and Weinshank and their shotguns drooping toward the floor and the complete lack of determination in their eyes. He accepted the math of the weaponry and lowered his gun.

Not good or fast enough as Giancana fired another quick burst, hitting May. The mechanic, who'd picked the wrong day to go to work, slammed against the brick wall and then slowly slid to the concrete floor, leaving a smear of blood. He was moaning in pain. He lifted a hand, searching for some succor. The German Shepherd tied to the bumper of the truck began barking.

Strings, carrying a gun pressed up against the base of Ivar's skull, entered the garage behind Giancana and Accardo.

"Geez, Sam," Strings said, briefly removing his pistol from the back of Ivar's head and firing twice, stopping the moaning. Then he aimed at the dog.

"Please don't," Scout said. "The dog hasn't hurt anyone."

"And it's supposed to live," Moms added.

Strings smiled. "So you know who lives and dies? Makes sense."

Clark was completely shaken, not just by the sudden reversal of fortune, but trying to process Moms' words. "What's going on?"

"Where's Moran?" Sam Giancana demanded, a few sentences behind.

"Not here," Moms said. She nodded at Ivar whose level of surprise at this turn of events was evident. "You all right?"

"What are you doing here?" Ivar asked.

Clark managed to regroup a little bit. He looked at Moms, then at the intruders. "You guys together? I knew it was a set up. Capone is a lying punk."

"What's going on, Strings?" Giancana asked. "Who are these other people? Where's Moran? Why'd you tell us he was here? Aint none of this making any sense."

Strings shoved Ivar towards Moms and Scout and took a step back, to a position to the side of Giancana and Accardo.

Moms finished tying the bandage even tighter. "Finger here," she asked Scout. She grimaced as she cinched the knot.

"Okay," Strings said. "Everyone is here." He counted. "Two dead. Okay, that's done." He holstered his .45 and went over to the steel canister containing the bomb. He pressed down on a specific point on the surface and a panel slid to the side. He reached in and retrieved a small clacker. He held it up so everyone could see. "Dead man's switch." He squeezed and the bomb beeped. "It's live. I let go of this switch, it finishes countdown and goes off. Kills everyone in here in five seconds. So nobody messes with me. Everybody got that?" He checked first with Giancana and Accardo. Both of the gangsters nodded, confused. Then Clark. Then the team.

"Don't you die too?" Accardo pointed out.

"Yeah," Strings agreed, "but it's a chance I'm willing to take."

"Mutually assured destruction," Eagle said.

"Huh?" Giancana said.

Giancana and Accardo were processing the situation, the muzzles of their Tommy-guns still pointed in the general direction of the team and Clark, Heyer and Weinshank.

"Who is this guy?" Moms asked Ivar.

"Supposedly the A-I-T," Ivar said. "He's the one who gets Lansky to write my letter. Later. But I think he's working for the other side."

"Duh," Scout muttered.

"What did you do to the A-I-T?" Moms asked Strings.

He threw his own question back at her. "Where's the Possibility Palace?"

"Don't know," Moms said. "None of us know."

"What are you guys talking about?" Giancana demanded.

"Shut up," Strings said.

A muscle twitched in anger on the side of Giancana's face, but he shut up.

Eagle spoke. "We don't have a need to know, so we don't know. You can understand that makes sense."

"How do you get to the Palace from the present?" Strings asked. "Your present? In your timeline? Where is the Gate?"

Moms shook her head. "I don't remember."

"Then I'm going to start killing your people one by one until someone tells me," Strings said. With his free hand, he drew his pistol. "Eenie, meenie, minie, mo," he intoned as he moved the muzzle from Moms, to Scout, to Eagle, to Roland, to Doc, to Ivar and then back to Moms, "catch, a, tiger—"

He paused as the door marked 'Private' opened.

"-by the toe," the waitress who'd warned Ivar finished. She was flanked on the left by Atropos in her white robe, long scissors in her arms and Clotho on the right in a black robe, leather-bound book in the crook of her arm.

Strings wheeled, bringing the .45 to bear on the Fates. Giancana and Accardo targeted them with their Thompsons.

Lachesis pulled a short, white rod out of the apron of her waitress uniform. "We will not be shot today."

And she wasn't as their fingers twitched on the triggers but couldn't pull.

Clotho held a hand up, spreading the fingers wide. The air in the garage crackled with energy and the interior walls of the garage shimmered with energy. The field also spread around Giancana and Accardo, freezing them. She announced: "No one is coming in and no one is coming out of here until it is fulfilled as it should be."

"And what should be?" Moms asked, forcing herself to her feet, Scout assisting her.

"The scales must be balanced," Lachesis said.

"Seven must be dead for this to end," Atropos confirmed.

The Space Between

Lara stood waist deep in the oily water of the lake, right next to the column rippled with blue and gold. Earhart was twenty feet away, on shore, her samurais deployed in a defensive semi-circle.

"Don't!" Earhart called out as Lara reached toward the shimmering surface of the column. "If it's not your Gate, it will burn you."

Lara nodded, then stuck her hand into the surface. In an instant, the surface of the column expanded around her, putting her in a flickering gold and blue blister. The dark water that hit the blister hissed and steamed.

*****

There's pain, but I know pain.

And it's darkness. Hello, my old friend.

Crap, where did I get that tune in my head? Where do I get all this stuff in my head?

She said I was made. Sarah. The sister who never existed. Who was she? She knew them. The ones who came for me. And my brother, the one I didn't know, but did exist. He was dying, but did he?

Pain. Here. Now.

My hand is on fire. Strange. So much pain, but the flesh remains.

There's confusion. Overlapping chatter, arguing, voices from the past echoing into the future.

The team.

My team? They're in trouble. What do I owe them? How far into the pain should I go? How much can I take?

Everything is black.

Just the pain.

Forms and shapes. I know this place. I know this fear.

Things are becoming clearer.

I'm in the kitchen.

This isn't good. This isn't where I want to be.

I need to leave.

I pull back, grab the thread back to the Space Between, the spirit of Amelia Earhart. Strong, brave, tangible.

I pause.

There is singing in the other room.

Warren Zevon.

Oh, I don't want to go there.

Really. Don't. Want. To.

I don't think so.

The Mission Phase V

Chicago, 14 February 1929 A.D.

Strings was the first to act on Fate's proclamation, shifting his aim and firing four times, two bullets at each target.

Adam Heyer and Albert Weinshank dropped unceremoniously to the pitted concrete floor.

"Over halfway there," Strings announced. He'd lost his Chicago gangster and was speaking with a strange accent, as if English was not his primary language. He aimed at Moms. "That is a compromise on my part. Now your turn to compromise. Tell me what I want, and some of your Team can go home."

"Why?" Moms said to the Fates. "Why do there have to be seven dead?"

"It is what it is," Atropos said. "The scales must be balanced inside the bubble. We did not make this. But we will confirm it."

"If *you* didn't make it," Moms asked, *"who* did?"

They didn't answer.

Strings looked at Moms. "I just helped you. Tell me what I want to know and most of your team can get out of here alive."

"What's with them?" Moms asked, indicating Accardo and Giancana.

Both gangsters were frozen, the field the Fates had propagated simmering around them.

"They are not part of this," Clotho said. "It is between you. The Shadow and the Patrol. It is the choices you have made and will make."

"They're not part of the decision-making," Moms indicated Accardo and Giancana, "but why don't we kill them?"

"I second that," Scout said. "Let's kill the psychopaths."

"I think it's a good idea," Ivar added.

Roland stirred, opened his eyes, took in the scenario, didn't say anything, glaring at Strings. Roland was always good at quickly sizing up a situation and focusing on the enemy. His muscles bulged as he worked on the ropes.

"We can't," Eagle said. He relied on more than just the download. He had his tremendous memory and his study of history readily available. "Accardo eventually runs the Outfit; the Chicago mob. He expands their power beyond Chicago into Vegas and the entire western United States."

"So he's a bad guy," Scout said.

"Yes," Eagle agreed. "Except think of how many people and events he affects? He dies now, it will be a ripple that would probably be a cascade."

"Or he's a murdering asshole no one will miss," Scout said.

"And Giancana?" Moms asked.

"Worse," Eagle said. "He shared a mistress, Judith Exner, with John F. Kennedy. Some say he directed the Outfit, at Joe Kennedy's request and bribe, to throw the 1960 Presidential election in Chicago, and thus Illinois, to Kennedy. That doesn't happen? What if Kennedy never becomes President? Definitely a cascade. Kennedy also approached Accardo about assassinating Castro."

"We have to kill someone?" Roland asked, eager for action, and behind the situation; which was not abnormal. He was still working the ropes; Roland could double-task on some things.

"But haven't we already caused a ripple," Doc said, "with them being here? Seeing us?"

Lachesis answered. "They will remember nothing of this. And, as noted, their fates are set and their thread will not be cut today. They are not a variable here."

Ivar and Doc exchanged a glance at that last sentence.

"And him?" Moms indicated Clark who wasn't covered by the field and isolated between the two groups.

"Hey!" Clark protested. "Al told me about the set up. He promised me I could walk."

"That's not in the history," Eagle noted.

"Yeah," Scout said. "Probably because this jerk double-crossed Moran with Capone and then Capone triple-crossed him and he got whacked."

"Well?" Moms asked the Fates.

"His thread is cut today," Atropos said.

"Al promised me!" Clark said.

"And you'll haunt him for the rest of his life," Doc said. "Your spirit won't find peace until he is dead. This won't be your forever death. Not yet."

"What the hell?" Clark said.

"Enough!" Strings yelled and then he fired, the round hitting Clark directly between the eyes, producing a small black hole. The exit wound, however, was a fountain of blood, bone and brains.

The German Shepherd whimpered and crawled further under the truck.

"Now we are down to only two have to die," Strings said. "A small sacrifice."

"Speak for yourself," Scout said.

Moms turned to the three Fates. "When this bubble collapses, what happens?"

Clotho fielded that. "If there are seven dead, as should be, all will be as it would have been. As soon as the seventh death occurs, you will all go back through your respective Gates. This bubble collapses."

Scout indicated Giancana and Accardo. "My vote is we whack those two guys."

"I have told you," Clotho said. "They are not part of this."

"If the bomb goes off," Scout said, "they're a dead variable."

"If the bomb goes off," Lachesis said, "they will not be harmed. The blast will be contained inside this bubble, excluding them. We are done here. You will be released when what has been written is what is."

The three Fates faded out and were gone.

"Gee, thanks," Scout said. "That was fraking helpful. Not."

Eagle spoke to Strings. "Legion?"

"No," Strings said.

"Sparta?" Moms asked, referring to the timeline ruled by Sparta that was in thrall to the Shadow, trading warriors for existence.

Strings straightened up, almost coming to attention. "Backhos, son of Hesiod. Twenty-third of my agoge to be sent to serve."

"Is that a bomb?" Roland asked, trying to catch up. With a snap, the rope parted and he was free. He stood up, flexing, readying for action.

"It is," Moms said, "and he has a dead man's switch. And the gun."

That Roland could process instantly. He gathered up his cutlass and boarding axe.

"But he's only got one bullet left," Scout noted. "Since the slide isn't back, indicating he's out of ammo, then he had one in the chamber and a full mag. Now he's down to one in the chamber. Nothing in the mag."

Roland smiled at Scout, giving her an A in weaponology.

Scout went to Eagle and began untying him.

"What are you doing?" Backhos demanded.

"Duh," Scout said. "What's it look like? You going to spend your last bullet on me? Do it and Moms and Roland and Ivar will take you out."

Backhos took a step back, assessing his tactical situation, pistol in one hand, clacker in the other. "I have the bomb."

"Yeah, yeah," Scout said, going to Doc. "Blow us all up. That's the smart solution. Got seven bodies and more then. No one goes back. And if you were gonna do that, you would have done it. So you don't want to do that. That's not your mission. You're here for information. Your boss, the Shadow, whoever the frak that is, put a lot of time and energy into setting this up. Could have killed all of us much easier; sent us through Gates into a volcano or something." She paused as a thought struck her. "But maybe it can't do that? Maybe the Fates won't allow something so simple?"

"The Fates are meddling trouble-makers," Backhos said. "No one knows why they do what they do."

"Yeah, whatever," Scout said. "But *you* want that info. Which means old Shadow, whoever or whatever that is, is getting desperate. You want to attack the Time Patrol directly. Killing the Team isn't enough. You got to take out the entire place."

"I believe," Ivar said, "that the Shadow has already taken out a Time Patrol team. The team before us. And it changed nothing."

"Except for the Team that got taken out," Scout pointed out.

Eagle was nodding. "We've been too successful, haven't we?"

Backhos shrugged. "I need the information. That's all I know."

"Just following orders?" Scout asked.

Roland had axe and cutlass at the ready. Eagle was moving to the side, spreading the team out.

"Six to one," Moms said.

"My contingency," Backhos said, "is to kill this Team. That will be satisfactory to the ledger between my people and the Shadow. I do this for the greater good of my people. For Sparta."

*****

LARA:

The songs are all that can get through.

I know that without knowing why I know that, which is pretty much the screwed up way I know a lot of things. Like I know the word fetid.

Really? Where did I hear that?

The problem, the thing that scares me worse than scared can be, is that I know for certain this isn't a dream.

This is real, real.

I've got to help the team.

I take a step. Of my own volition, toward that door.

Another.

I don't think so.

I do think so.

Another.

I'm there. I reach up. My hand is shaking. Even in this, I can't appear brave? Resolute?

There it is, another word. Where did I get that one from? Was that in Moms' corny speech about manning the wall and all that other stuff?

Yeah, yeah, I can live with that.

Probably die with it too.

I push the door open. It swings both ways. How come I never focused on that before?

A couple of inches. I peek inside.

Oh My God!

I don't think so.

*****

"Until when?" Moms asked.

Backhos frowned. "What?"

"Until when?" Moms repeated. "Will Sparta serve the Shadow forever? What happens if the Shadow is successful and no longer needs your timeline's service? The better you fight, the quicker your people, your timeline, will be annihilated."

"I do as my King orders," Backhos said.

"I fought with a Spartan king," Scout said. "King Leonidas."

"Leonidas fought many battles," Backhos said.

"I was at his side at Thermopylae," Scout said.

"In my timeline," Backhos said, "no Spartan survived Thermopylae."

"None did in our timeline either," Scout said. "I'm not a Spartan. But Leonidas, and his men, sacrificed themselves. So that I could fulfill my mission. *He* was a Spartan King. I can't see him bowing his head to the Shadow."

"Leonidas was a great King," Backhos allowed. "But that doesn't matter. In the end we lost to the Shadow and have done what we need to in order to live. I have my orders."

"Geez," Scout muttered. "He's your kind of guy, Roland."

*****

LARA:

A man is standing in there, a knife in his hand, blood dripping from the blade.

I'm not too late like I thought before. I will be never be too late for this room and this man. He will always be in there waiting for me. There will always be blood dripping from his blade.

He is Joey, from the diner in Boise. He is Legion, from the Fifth Floor.

He is death.

"Where you going, kid?"

There are bodies on the floor, but I know they're not my family. The family I never had. I don't want to know who they are; whose blood drips from his blade.

He points over his shoulder to the front door and whatever is beyond it. "You wanna go that way? Go ahead."

He will kill me. He's designed to kill. It is his only purpose.

I know all those things as surely as I know anything, which isn't much, but, okay, more than I know most things.

I know he will kill me.

"You're all alone, kid," he says, smiling.

The team.

But I can't.

I am alone.

I want to. I want to. But it's like when I want to wake up from the dream.

I can't.

I need a dream line. A thread to grab hold of.

I hear the songs and there is a vision: the team, in a garage, with others.

That is enough for me to understand the situation; how it all hangs in the balance.

I have to go past Joey, through the front door.

And then further.

I can't do it.

I just can't.

I hear a whine.

He, Joey, hears it too. He's confused.

A dog.

A dog?

There was a dog.

There is a dog.

*****

"I do have one bullet left," Backhos said. "But that will not be enough to release the hold the Fates have placed on us."

"Then you're screwed," Scout said.

"No," Backhos said. "You are. Even if you kill me, there is the bomb. And there is the hold. One more must die for you to escape. That cannot be argued with or changed."

Roland strode up to Giancana and swung the boarding axe. It hit the field around the gangster and bounced off, causing no damage.

"I took the old women at their word," Backhos said. "They are the Fates."

"Why are they interfering?" Moms asked.

Backhos shrugged. "They are not. They are making sure the scales are balanced."

"That's bull," Scout said. "The Shadow is trying to change history. To unbalance the scales. But the Fates only stick their nose in once in a while. Seems they would stop the Shadow all the time."

"Perhaps," Backhos said. "I don't pretend to understand the ways of the Gods."

"The Fates aren't Gods," Eagle said.

"What are they then?" Backhos asked. "None of that matters. Tell me what I want to know or all will die. The Fates will be satisfied and the Time Patrol will all be dead."

*****

Not all.

"Come," Joey waves the bloody knife at the front door. "Your friends need help."

He isn't a good salesman, using that knife to point. I remember him cutting those pies in Boise. I should have paid better attention.

Highball.

Who names a dog after a drink?

Scout?

*****

"We are also warriors," Moms said. "We will die before we tell you anything that will harm our timeline. We both have the same thing at stake, except our timeline is fighting the Shadow. Yours is in thrall to it."

"Poor doggie," Scout said, walking toward the truck and the cowering German Shepherd.

"What are you doing?" Backhos demanded.

"The dog is scared," Scout said. She knelt next to Highball and untied the rope from around his neck. "There. Good boy."

"I will not yield," Backhos said to Moms.

Everyone was surprised when Scout began to hum. It took the other team members only a few seconds to understand.

Moms was first to sing. *"Roland was a warrior from the Land of the Midnight Sun."*

Scout closed her eyes.

Roland readied his weapons as Eagle and Doc joined Moms for the second line, none of them having a clue what Scout was doing. *"With a Thompson gun for hire—"* and then the room slowed.

For everyone but Scout, and Highball, because Scout's hand was on his neck.

"f-i-g-h-t-i-n-g----- t—o-------- b---e-----------d----o----n----e."

Scout went for Backhos, Highball at her side. Backhos reacted, far too slow in the altered time sense, but faster than non-Spartan trained humans. But not as fast as a Legion, and Scout had managed to shoot one charging at her on her last mission.

Scout's hand clamped down on Backhos' gun hand, jamming her thumb between the hammer and rear of the slide and shoving the aim away from Moms.

Highball, Scout's hand still on his neck, leapt. His teeth locked down on Backhos' hand holding the clacker.

"T-----h-----e---------- d------e------a------l

And then time resumed its normal cadence.

"Was made—"

They stopped singing as everyone took in the tableau. Highball's teeth a vise on the hand and the clacker it held. Scout let go of Highball and ripped the gun out of Backhos'. She stepped back, gun in hand.

"Everyone all right?"

"How did you get the dog—" Moms wondered.

"I didn't," Scout said. "Lara did. She told me."

Backhos was in pain, but barely showed it, true Spartan to the end. "I can kill the dog." He drew a dagger with his free hand. "And then we are back to—"

He didn't finish the statement as Scout fired. He died instantly.

"We need to secure the clacker," Moms said.

"It is secured," Scout said. "We're still not out of this."

"One more death," Doc said. "One more before we can go back." He walked over to Giancana and Accardo. "They are off limits. So it must be one of us."

"Unacceptable," Moms said.

Highball's growl was beginning to shift to a whine, but he was still holding the dead hand in his jaws.

*****

Let's move it, people.

I can't keep this up forever.

I can see Joey. He's so smooth. He could have been a ballet dancer.

How the frak do I know ballet? I've never been to one. Never seen one.

He's not going to kill me.

How do I know that?

Because killing would be too easy. He has something much worse in mind for me.

Because the Shadow has something much worse for me.

Come on, guys! Do something.

I gotta get out of here.

*****

"Numbers," Doc said. He picked up one of the discarded shotguns. "It is math and you cannot argue with math. Or fate." He smiled sadly as he said the last. "More correctly, the Fates. They have decreed seven must die."

"No," Moms said.

"What are you doing?" Roland was concerned and a beat behind.

Scout had her head cocked to the side. "We don't have much time. Lara is in trouble. She's holding the dog in place, but . . ."

Doc looked at Ivar. "You know math. You have a possible answer now in math for the attacks. Maybe it's correct. Maybe not. But the math here is irrefutable." He sat down, placing the muzzle of the shotgun under his chin.

"No," Moms said.

"Scout," Doc called out.

"Yes?"

"Here." He tossed her an old pair of spectacles. "They were Benjamin Franklin's."

*****

If I move, Highball let's go. The dog is scared.

Join the club, buddy.

Joey slashes at me with his knife.

A thin slice on my cheek.

Was it real? The pain felt like it.

They briefed me on Legion. They're cutters. Not like the cutters I knew on the First Floor. Legion cuts others. They take pride in how many they can inflict before their victim dies.

That's pretty fraked up.

"You feel it," Joey said.

"Nah."

"You lie poorly."

He cuts me again.

Let's do something people!

"Want some more pie?" Joey asks.

*****

"She can't hold much longer," Scout said, moving next to Highball and extending her hands to grab the clacker in case the dog lets go.

Eagle was next to Moms. "He's right," the team sergeant said. "We have no choice."

"I'm dying," Doc said. "The radiation from the D-Day mission. The meds Dane passed to me only gave me more time. Not a solution. There is only one inevitability. I would prefer to go on my own terms. And not the way those who were exposed to the Demon Core went. That is a horrible, slow, death."

"No." Moms was adamant. "There has to be another way."

"Prepare to move quickly," Doc said. "Keep me in your hearts."

He pulled the trigger.

*****

I run for the door back to the kitchen.

"Stay!" Joey screamed.

I'm through. Someone has a hand one my shoulder, pulling me back.

I snap into Space Between. Amelia Earhart has me in her arms, waist deep in the oil water of the lake.

*****

Highball let go of the clacker as six Gates opened.

.04

"Go!" Moms ordered.

Roland, as usual, was first, because an order from Moms was always obeyed instantly. He went through his Gate, axe and cutlass in hand.

.03

Scout saw the number on the bomb, reached for the clacker.

"No, Scout," Moms said.

Ivar went through his Gate.

.02

Scout jumped for her Gate and was gone.

.01

Moms and Eagle were both gone.

The Return

The samurai went to one knee in unison and bowed their heads toward Lara.

"What's this?" she asked.

"They are giving you respect and honor," Earhart said. "For what you did."

I didn't go through the front door, Lara thought. *And Doc is dead because of that.*

"I have to get back," Lara said.

"Of course." Earhart indicated the way along the beach to get near the location of the Gate to return.

*****

ASCENDING INTO THE TUNNEL OF TIME, IVAR saw the explosion, a flash that blinded him for a moment.

Then there was the interior of the garage. Unmarred by an explosion. Seven bodies splayed out as they had been in the photos in the download. As they had been in history.

It was all as it should be, just as the Fates had decreed.

As the interior the garage begin to fade away in the distance, Ivar heard a faint sound and smiled.

Highball barking.

*****

EAGLE was speeding through the tunnel of time, moving forward, the planet blurring below him, but he abruptly slowed, coming to almost a standstill high above a ship he immediately recognized.

The *USS Quincy*. Steaming in the open ocean under a full moon. On the deck, President Franklin D. Roosevelt sat alone at the very bow, a blanket over his lap. Several crewmen hovered a discreet distance away, prepared to assist in any way needed.

Because Major General 'Pa' Watson, West Point class of 1908, was dead. Cerebral hemorrhage. That's what the history books would record.

Eagle wasn't so sure.

Roosevelt had a folder in his hands.

Eagle squinted, seeing through the wall of the tunnel, but not quite seeing. Still, he knew what it was. The Top Secret targeting folder for the Manhattan Project. Something that had only partially been made public in Eagle's time.

The section on the German targeting, Berlin at the top of the list, had been redacted.

Hiroshima.

Nagasaki.

Something fell on the page.

Eagle realized it was a single tear.

Then Roosevelt snapped the folder shut.

*****

IN THE TUNNEL OF TIME, ROLAND remembered the Jager he'd fought Grendel beside, asking: *How much is any man's life worth?*

A life is worth only the lives it can take, was the proper Jager answer.

Roland had not believed that.

A life is worth the lives it loves, not those it kills.

And now, Roland had to add to that.

A life is worth the lives it saves.

Distantly, without much interest, he could see a melee on the beach of Kealakekua Bay. Captain Cook was stabbed in the back, running for the boat, falling into the surf. Knives plunged into him.

All was as it should be in history.

*****

MOMS was in the tunnel of time.

Numb. Barely interested in the flash of bulbs outside the tunnel as reporters covered the public revealing of ENIAC.

The ENIAC Six, so crucial to the programming and maintenance of the machine, were off to the side. Basically ignored.

But they were there.

And the machine was too.

Technology would march on.

Moms didn't care.

*****

SCOUT was in the tunnel of time, trying to understand.

The Earth was flashing below her. Years going by. A bright flash on each 14 February. Valentines Day. When people professed love, having little idea of the roots of the day.

Love?

Greater love hath no man than this: that a man lay down his life for his friends.

She had no idea where that came from. It sounded Biblical or something Eagle would conjure up from his vast trove of knowledge.

She looked at the spectacles in her hands.

Far below was the Milvian Bridge. A glittering cluster of metal objects adorned the edge, right where Valentine had been killed. Scout didn't recognize them at first, then realized they were padlocks.

Love padlocks.

To symbolize unbreakable love.

Keep me in your heart for a while.

*****

DOC was there and he wasn't there.

I shouldn't be anywhere.

"You did well."

Atropos was to his left. All else was just a gray nothingness.

"Is this death?"

"It is what it is."

Helpful as usual. Doc could hear Scout: *Not*

"What was all this?" Doc asked. "Just the Shadow trying to locate the Time Patrol base?"

"You know better than that," Atropos said. She was dressed in a white robe, the scissors in the crook of her arm. Her hood was pulled back, revealing a lined and wrinkled face. Her eyes were pure white. She reached. "Come with me."

"Where?"

"Does it matter? Besides, you have no choice now. You are on a different plane."

Doc took her hand. Her skin was dry and cool to the touch.

Something flitted by to the left, startling Doc.

"It is just the restless spirit of one who you saw die."

"Clark?"

"He will haunt the man who betrayed him until satisfaction in that man's death."

Capone was going to have some hard times ahead. Doc had no sympathy.

"What about my teammates?"

"They are back."

"What of Kurt Vonnegut?" Doc asked. "My mission."

"You saved him."

"This was a test," Doc said. "You tested us."

"It is what it is," Clotho said.

There was something ahead. Something Doc couldn't make out in the grey, but it was brighter. "What is that? Where are you taking me?"

"You have proved your worth," Atropos said.

Then Doc saw the truth. "Math wouldn't work to prove this.

Atropos smiled. "Not the math you know. So far."

The Possibility Palace

Where? Can't Tell You. When? Can't Tell You.

Lara stood on the edge of the Pit, staring aimlessly into its depths.

The others were in the team room, debriefing from the mission, grieving the loss of Doc, grateful to have survived.

A mixture of emotions Lara could feel, sharp and brittle, pushing through the cacophony of the 'voices' in the Pit.

Hold me in your thoughts.

Take me to your dreams.

Lara swallowed. That was Scout. With whom she had the strongest connection. More than a dream-line.

Lara could never take Scout there. Not through that door.

Here there be monsters.

Lara was startled as a competing voice pierced out of the Pit.

And her immediate thought was one of redemption: *If there be monsters, bring them on!*

The End
For Now

Our History Afterward

Chicago, 14 February 1929 A.D.

Seven men were killed in the St. Valentines Day Massacre. Public outrage over the killings increased pressure on the mob. No one was ever arrested for the killings and their identity is still a mystery.

Al Capone was widely suspected to be behind the killings. He was haunted by visions of Jimmy Clark until he died; it's suspected these came from his mind deteriorating from syphilis. He was arrested for tax evasion by Elliott Ness and imprisoned. He was paroled in 1939. He lived in Florida, his mind failing, until his death in 1947.

The Great Bitter Lake, 14 February 1945 A.D.

Most attention at the time, and in history, has focused on the Yalta Conference and its aftereffects.

Roosevelt's meeting with King Ibn Saud was, and still is, considered a footnote. However, This meeting had grave implications to the present day in shaping U.S. policy in the Middle East. While Roosevelt had supported a Zionist State in the Middle East, King Saud was strongly opposed to this. Taken aback by the King's strong reaction, Roosevelt backed off pushing the issue. He was dead on 12 April 1945.

The issue continues to haunt the world to this day.

Hawaii, 14 February 1779 A.D.

Captain Cook is on the list of great explorers. He was the first European to land on the east coast of Australia and also Hawaii. He circumnavigated New Zealand. He explored the Pacific Northwest Coast of North America.

On 14 February 1779, in an altercation with native Hawaiians, Cook was killed.

Despite the altercation, the islanders held Cook in high esteem. They prepared his body with their traditional funeral rights for chiefs. They disemboweled him, cooked the flesh off, and cleaned his bones. Some of the bones were returned to his crew for burial at sea.

Cook was so well renowned in his time, that during the American Revolution, Benjamin Franklin had a letter sent to American Naval captains that if they encountered Cook's vessel, they were not to attack it and to treat him as a 'friend to mankind'. Unfortunately, this letter was written a month after Cook's death.

One of his sailors, William Bligh, survived the journey and went to a bit of infamy with the USS Bounty.

Dresden, Germany, 14 February 1945 A.D.

The firebombing of Dresden remains controversial to this day. The necessity for the raid is constantly questioned. Numbers of casualties ranged from 30,000 to 200,000 although the figure has generally been agreed upon at 25,000.

There are many who felt the city had little military value and thus the attack was unnecessary. Others believe it was war and any target was valid. At the time of the bombing, Dresden was the seventh largest German city and the largest not to have been attacked. In a way, that made it a target as the city was filled with workers, troops and refugees.

Some believe it was a war crime, or, at the very least, immoral.

Kurt Vonnegut survived the raid and went on to write *Slaughterhouse Five*. It contains scenes set in Dresden. He described the bombing as 'carnage unfathomable.' He was assigned a detail burying the bodies.

Italy, 14 February 278 A.D.

According to legend, St. Valentine was an early priest who insisted on marrying couples despite the Emperor's edict against it. He was ordered to renounce his faith or be executed. He refused to renounce.

The romantic aspect of the day probably began in the Middle Ages, partly because it was believed that birds paired in couples in mid-February and also because of writings by Chaucer. The holiday might also have been invented to overcome the pagan holiday of Lupercalia.

There are relics of St. Valentine all over the world. His flower-adorned skull is supposedly in the Basilica of Santa Maria in Cosmedin Rome. An Irish priest was given a vial said to contain St. Valentines' blood by Pope Gregory XVI in 1836 and now resides in a church in Dublin.

St. Valentine is the patron saint of engaged couples, epilepsy, fainting, happy marriages, bee keepers, plague, lovers and young people.

Philadelphia PA, 14 February 1946

The unveiling of the ENIAC, previously kept classified because it was also used in calculations for the Manhattan project, made the front page of the NY Times after it was unveiled on Valentines Day with the headline: *Electronic Computer Flashes Answers, May Speed Engineering.*

ENIAC Six, largely ignored in history, not only helped program and keep that computer running; they showed that programming was as essential in the field as the hardware. They also helped develop the concept of subroutines and nested subroutines. One of the group, Jean Jennings Bartik, just before she died in 2011, said: *"Despite our coming of age in an era when women's career opportunities were generally quite confined, we helped initiate the era of the computer."*

The Next Book in the Time Patrol series is HALLOWS EVE

An Excerpt follows author and books information

AMAZON

The next book in the 2 million copy Area 51 series, **Resurrection** will be published in Winter 2017.

The next in the million copy selling Green Beret series, **Old Soldiers**, will be published Spring 2018.

About the Author

Thanks for the read!
If you enjoyed the book, please leave a review. Cool Gus likes them as much as he likes squirrels!
Any questions or comments, feel free to email me at bob@bobmayer.com
Subscribe to my newsletter for the latest news, free eBooks, audio, etc.

Look! Squirrel!
Bob is a NY Times Bestselling author, graduate of West Point, former Green Beret and the feeder of two Yellow Labs, most famously Cool Gus. He's had over 70 books published including the #1 series Area 51, Atlantis, Time Patrol and The Green Berets. Born in the Bronx, having traveled the world (usually not tourist spots), he now lives peacefully with his wife, and labs. He's training his two grandsons to be leaders of the Resistance Against The Machines.

For information on all my books, please get a free copy of my **Reader's Guide**. You can download it in mobi (Amazon) ePub (iBooks, Nook, Kobo) or PDF, from my home page at www.bobmayer.com

For free eBooks, short stories and audio short stories, please go to
http://bobmayer.com/freebies/
Free books include:
Eyes of the Hammer (Green Beret series book #1)
West Point to Mexico (Duty, Honor, Country series book #1)
Ides of March (Time Patrol)
Prepare Now-Survive Now
There are also free shorts stories and free audiobook stories.

Never miss a new release by following my Amazon Author Page.

I have over 220 free, downloadable Powerpoint presentations via Slideshare on a wide range of topics from history, to survival, to writing, to book trailers.
https://www.slideshare.net/coolgus

If you're interested in audiobooks, you can download one for free and test it out here:
Audible

Connect with me and Cool Gus on social media.
Blog: http://bobmayer.com/blog/
Twitter: https://twitter.com/Bob_Mayer

CONNECTIONS BETWEEN SERIES VIA PLOT AND CHARACTERS:
Technically the first *Time Patrol* book is the fourth *Nightstalker* book. You can start the Time Patrol series with Time Patrol, but if you want to know about what they did before, as Nightstalkers, then those three books show that.
The Fifth Floor is part of Time Patrol, but different in that it's the backstory of one of the characters: Lara.
The universe of *Atlantis* is the same as that in *Time Patrol* with the Shadow trying to change a timeline. They are just different timelines. Thus we have characters from Atlantis such as Dane and Foreman showing up in the Time Patrol.
The *Cellar* becomes involved in the *Nightstalkers* and *Time Patrol*, with Hannah and Neeley playing roles.

NIGHSTALKERS SERIES:
1. NIGHTSTALKERS
2. BOOK OF TRUTHS
3. THE RIFT
The fourth book in the Nightstalker book is the team becoming the Time Patrol, thus it's labeled book 4 in that series but it's actually book 1 in the Time Patrol series.

TIME PATROL SERIES:
1. TIME PATROL
2. BLACK TUESDAY
3. IDES OF MARCH *(free)*
4. D-DAY
5. INDEPENDENCE DAY
6. THE FIFTH FLOOR
7. NINE-ELEVEN
8. VALENTINES DAY
9. HALLOWS EVE

AREA 51 SERIES:

1. AREA 51
2. AREA 51 THE REPLY
3. AREA 51 THE MISSION
4. AREA 51 THE SPHINX
5. AREA 51 THE GRAIL
6. AREA 51 EXCALIBUR
7. AREA 51 THE TRUTH
(Legend and Nosferatu are prequels to the main series)
8. AREA 51 LEGEND
9. AREA 51 NOSFERATU
10. AREA 51 REDEMPTION (coming Winter 2018)

ATLANTIS SERIES:
1. ATLANTIS
2. ATLANTIS BERMUDA TRIANGLE
3. ATLANTIS DEVILS SEA
4. ATLANTIS GATE
5. ASSAULT ON ATLANTIS
6. BATTLE FOR ATLANTIS

THE GREEN BERETS SERIES:
1. EYES OF THE HAMMER *(free)*
2. DRAGON SIM-13
3. SYNBAT
4. CUT OUT
5. ETERNITY BASE
6. Z: FINAL COUNTDOWN
(at this point we introduce Horace Chase as the main character and he eventually teams up with Dave Riley, the main character from the previous books)
7. CHASING THE GHOST
8. CHASING THE LOST
9. CHASING THE SON
10. OLD SOLDIERS (coming spring 2018)

THE DUTY, HONOR, COUNTRY SERIES

THE SHADOW WARRIORS SERIES

THE PRESIDENTIAL SERIES

THE CELLAR SERIES

THE BURNERS SERIES

THE PSYCHIC WARRIOR SERIES

COLLABORATIONS WITH JENNIFER CRUSIE

All my novels and series are listed in order, with links here:
www.bobmayer.com/fiction/

My nonfiction, including my two companion books for preparation and survival is listed at
www.bobmayer.com/nonfiction/

Thank you!

Hallows Eve

A TIME PATROL NOVEL

"I'm not superstitious. I'm a witch. Witches aren't superstitious. We are what people are superstitious of."

Terry Pratchett

Where The Time Patrol Ended Up This Particular Day: 31 October

"Up! Children of Zulu, your day has come. Up! And destroy them all." Shaka Zulu
Zululand, Africa, 31 October 1828 A.D.

"I take that as no." Shaka slammed the *iklwa* into the old witch's chest, pinning her to the ground. She squirmed, then went still.

"Come here, spy," Shaka said, gesturing for Eagle to approach his throne composed of human bones. "There is something I want to show you. Perhaps in your treasonous life, you have seen something like it."

Eagle knew he stood no chance against Shaka, *iklwa* to *iklwa*, regardless of the Naga blade on his own. He walked forward, skirting around the dead woman.

Shaka lifted something heavy and tossed it toward Eagle. It thudded and rolled once.

It is 1828 A.D. Russia declares war on Turkey in support of Greek independence; Shaka Zulu, the most powerful Zulu ruler, dies (maybe); South Carolina declares the right of states to nullify Federal law; a storm off of Gibraltar sinks over 100 ships; Noah Webster publishes the first American dictionary; Simon Bolivar becomes dictator of Venezuela; Andrew Jackson is elected the seventh President of the United States with 642,553 votes after having not been named President in the 1824 election despite receiving the most electoral votes.

"What is that?" Shaka demanded.

Eagle knew why he was here.

Some things change; some don't.

"That, great King, is the head of a mighty beast we call a Grendel. And if there is one, there is at least one more like it. Larger, more dangerous. Capable of giving birth to many, many more."

Shaka laughed, a jagged edge to it. "At least *one* more? In the valley of the dead to the west, there are dozens of these beasts, guarding a watering hole. It was a mighty fight to get this one head. They were sent here to torment me in my grief."

"Until an hour before the Devil fell, God thought him beautiful in Heaven."
Arthur Miller, *The Crucible*
Salem Massachusetts, 31 October 1692 A.D.

"I really thought—" Pandora began, but she paused, cocking her head. "Do you have the Sight?" Her voice was lower, almost a whisper.

"Sort of," Lara said.

"Do you sense him?"

Lara *did* sense something or someone. In the forest. Moving. Coming this way. She'd felt this presence before; even met it.

"Joey," she whispered.

"Who is Joey?" Pandora said, turning in the direction of the presence, lifting her Naga to the ready. "They are all Legion. They don't have names."

"He is darkness," Lara said. "Evil."

It is 1692 A.D. The world's population is roughly 710 million with 436 million of those in Asia; Diego de Vargas, and Spanish colonists, retake Santa Fe, New Mexico from the Pueblo people after 12 years of exile and the event is still celebrated in the city; in February, the first people are accused of witchcraft in Salem: Sarah Good, Sarah Osborne, and Tituba; an earthquake devastates Jamaica and the resulting tsunami kills two to three thousand and destroys the capital, Port Royal; a Chinese Emperor issues the edict of Toleration, recognizing all Roman Catholic priests (not just Jesuits) and legalizing their right to convert Chinese; on June 10th the first to be hanged in Salem is Bridget Bishop.

"You do have some Sight," Pandora acknowledged. She lowered the point of her Naga staff slightly. "It is going away. But it knows we're here."

Some things change; some don't.

"Why didn't it attack?" Lara asked. She'd drawn her Naga dagger without consciously realizing it.

"It is not here for us," Pandora said.

"Who is it here for?"

"I truly expected it to be Scout that was chosen for this mission," Pandora said.

"Why is that?" Lara asked.

"Because if you fail in this mission, Scout will cease to exist."

"Every man must do two things alone; he must do his own believing and his own dying."
Martin Luther
Wittenberg, Germany, 31 October 1517 A.D.

Legion put one blade to his lips and licked it. "Your blood is indeed sweet. Are you a virgin?"

"Are you serious?" Scout said. "I think—" and she darted to her right, jumping onto a pew, and continuing up into the air.

No one ever looks up, Nada had always preached.

It is 1517 A.D. The Ottoman Empire captures Cairo, deposing the Mamluk Sultanate; the first official diplomatic mission of a European country to China is made in Hong Kong; the 1st Duke of Suffolk is born; Pope Leo X signs the 5th Council of Lateran covering such things as Church allowing pawn shops to give loans to the poor.

Of course, that was kind of worthless given Legion was completely focused on her. But her focus on time was everything and the world was slowing down once more. She could feel the wood under her sandal, her muscles contracting, expanding, pushing her up. She twisted aware of the air brushing against her skin, the musty odor of the church, and most of all, Legion turning, bringing one blade up to parry, the other ready to thrust upward and gut her.

Some things change; some don't.

But he was too slow as the tip of Scout's Naga dagger drew a thin red line along the side of his scalp starting at the temple, slicing through his ear, and ending at the back of the neck.

Scout landed on her feet. "That was pretty cool. Didn't know I could do that."

"I am alive today. I may not be here tomorrow."
Indira Gandhi (on 30 October, the night before her assassination)
New Delhi, 31 October 1984 A.D.

"I am Indira. And you are?"

"Neeley, Prime Minister."

"There is no need to be formal, is there?" Gandhi asked. "Not now. Not this evening, actually very early morning as the clock has already passed the midnight hour into a new day."

"Yes ma'am," Neeley said, a cup of tea cooling on the table in front of her, while the Prime Minister of India took a sip from her own cup. A gun rested on Neeley's lap, hidden by the tablecloth.

"Indira, please. And is Neeley your first name or surname?"

"It's just my name."

"Curious. Surely you were born with a full name?"

"I was."

Gandhi held up a hand. "I sense the issue is one that is sensitive to you. Forgive my intrusion. Neeley. Most interesting. You sound American, but there is a trace of an accent in your English. Having grown up here but being schooled in Europe, I have heard many accents. A bit of French perhaps?"

"I lived there for a while," Neeley admitted.

"Ah, France," Gandhi said. "Joan d'Arc. A true hero."

It is 1984 A.D. Cirque Du Soleil is founded; a 19 year old goes into a deep coma after an auto accident—he'll come out of it in 2003; Vanessa Williams becomes the first African-American to become Miss America, but it doesn't last; the IRA attempts to assassinate Prime Minister Thatcher and the British Cabinet with a bomb; Galileo is formally forgiven by the Vatican for his theory on the Earth's orbit, a bit late for him; Ronald Reagan is elected President; Apple introduces the Mac with an iconic commercial; the Winter Olympics are held in Sarajevo; crack cocaine is introduced in Los Angeles; Chrysler introduces the first mini-van (yay?); ; Iran accuses Iraq of using chemical weapons.

Gandhi looked down. "And you brought a gun."

Neeley put the pistol on the table. "For protection."

Some things change. Some don't.

"Really? And you know how to use it?"

"I do."

Gandhi took a sip of tea, reminding Neeley of her own. "This is very nice."

"My own mixture," Gandhi said. "Tea is such a strange symbol in my country. We produce it and the British exploited us for it. It seems everything in life cuts both ways. Now we no longer have the British but we still have our tea."

Neeley was never one for small talk so she didn't say anything.

Gandhi indicated the pistol. "Will you shoot me with that?"

*"Have you heard of a ship called the good Reuben James
Manned by hard fighting men both of honor and fame?"*
Woody Guthrie
The North Atlantic, 31 October 1941 A.D.

"Who are you?" the man hissed, leaning close, putting pressure on the blade at Roland's neck.

"Roland."

"Are you friend or foe?"

Roland slowly moved his left hand toward the handle of his dagger. "Friend or foe of who?" Roland asked as the destroyer *USS Reuben James* rolled steeply, a North Atlantic wave tossing the four-stack destroyer about.

"I was told one out of time would come," the man said. "I felt the disturbance of your arrival. Why are you here?"

Roland answered as carefully, and vaguely, as he could, which wasn't hard for him to do. "To make sure everything happens as it should."

It is 1941 A.D. Elmer's Pet Rabbit, aka Bugs Bunny, premiers; FDR is sworn in for his third term as President; all persons born in Puerto Rico henceforth will be U.S. Citizens; Grand Coulee Dam begins to generate electricity; Citizen Kane *premiers; Z3, the world's first working programmable automatic computer is introduced in Berlin; Joe DiMaggio begins his 56 game hitting streak; the first major airborne assault in history is launched by the Germans on Crete; Goring direct Heydrich to draw up plans for the Final Solution with Himmler to be in charge; the first Jeep rolls off the production line; the T4 program is initiated by the Nazis, euthanizing people with disabilities; Jews in the occupied territories must wear a Star of David; construction of the Pentagon building begins; German troops can see the steeples of Moscow, much as*

Napoleon had a century before, but it's snowing and cold, much like Napoleon experienced; Hong Kong falls to the Japanese; a breakfast called Cheerios is released.

The man laughed without mirth. "What *should* happen? You know? What do you know?"

"This ship sinks."

Some things change; some don't.

"*'This* ship sinks'?" The man was incredulous. "Who cares about *this* ship? It's the other ship, the submarine that we have to worry about. *That's* the one we have to destroy."

! ! ! Attention government sponsors of cyber warfare and those who profit from it ! ! !
Beginning of Patebin Page of the Shadow Brokers
ZERO DAY

The Gunman shot the guy in the Fedex outfit in the left eye. The slice of pizza he'd been holding hit the floor with a splat. Fedex man slumped in the seat, dead before he was aware he was going to die.

"No double-tap?" Ivar asked, trying to remain calm.

"No need, as you can clearly see."

"Right. I was taught double-tap."

"You were taught correctly," Gunman said, "but situations differ." He waggled the gun, which was now pointed at Ivar. "Twenty-two High Standard. A classic. One shot, eyeball, is enough. But you must be very accurate. The eye socket is a small target."

"Right." Ivar swallowed. "And now?"

It is Now. Zero Day in Zero Year. How we got to be here? 1801: Joseph Marie invents a loom using wood punch cards to weave certain fabric designs, the forerunner of computer punch cards; 1822: Charles Babbage conceptualizes a calculator powered by steam and is funded by the British Government, but his project fails; 1890: Herman Hollerith designs a punch system, not a machine, to help calculate the 1880 census and accomplishes the task in only three years (done by hand it took seven); the company he starts will eventually be known as IBM; 1936: Alan Turing conceptualizes a 'universal machine' that would be capable of computing anything that is computable, which is the essence of a computer. Sort of.

"We had an incident," Gunman said. "Excuse me. I have failed to introduce myself. I am Victor."

"'Victor'?" Ivar nodded. "Sure. Victor. I'm Ivar."

Some things change; some don't.

"As I was saying, we had an incident a while back. In the Negev."

This was worse than the mob, Ivar realized. *The fraking Israelis.*

"Someone appeared. Like you did. Caused great damage. I read the report. I broke protocol on my mission here because to understand what happened there and then is a higher priority than our surveillance here and now, although we believe the two might be connected." He pointed the pistol with the stubby suppressor directly at Ivar's left eye. "How did you get here?"

Hallows Eve (Time Patrol)

Copyright
Cool Gus Publishing

Cool Gus Publishing
coolgus.com

http://coolgus.com

Acknowledgements: Thanks to Ken Kendall and Dalice Peterson for their Beta Reads.

Valentines Day by Bob Mayer
COPYRIGHT © 2017 by Bob Mayer

Printed in Great Britain
by Amazon